Caffeine N

DEATH RUN

HARRY DUNN

For Jan and James
with My Very Best Wishes

Harry Dunn

Fiction aimed at the heart
and the head..

Published by Caffeine Nights Publishing 2019

Published in Great Britain by
Caffeine Nights Publishing
4 Eton Close
Walderslade
Chatham
Kent
ME5 9AT
www. caffeinenights com

British Library Cataloguing in Publication Data.
A CIP catalogue record for this book is available from the British Library

ISBN: 978-1-913200-00-8

Everything else by
Default, Luck and Accident

Harry was born into a journalistic family in Aberdeen. Educated at Robert Gordon's College, he went on to work in newspapers in several UK locations within the Thomson Organisation.

In 1967 he joined the BBC's Publications Division and was involved in their fast growing business of book publishing. When based in Leeds, he accompanied many celebrity authors on promotional tours throughout the North and this encouraged his love of reading during the many hours spent in hotels. His genre of choice was always crime and he carried a picture of the type of character he would one day have as a private investigator.

Thus was born the endearing character Jack Barclay and to quote Raymond Chandler:

'In everything that is called art there is a quality of redemption.....but down these mean streets a man must go who is not himself mean, who is neither tarnished nor afraid.'

Jack Barclay qualifies as a man who can walk these mean streets.

Harry has drawn on countless life experiences to help create a tense, fast paced and highly entertaining novel.

He is married with two grown up children and lives with his wife in Berkshire where he is a member of a thriving local writers group.

Widely travelled, he is also a frequent visitor to London's theatres and galleries and enjoys wandering around observing life in the Capital. This is balanced by visits to the sea where he loves to write. His golf handicap remains stubbornly in the high twenties.

Acknowledgements

Special thanks to my wonderful friend, editor and fellow author, Judy Bryan for her help and guidance.

My thanks also to Joanne Colby, Jo Davies and to members of the Wokingham Writers Group. We meet in the Wokingham Library, a much-loved place

To my family I send my thanks for their constant support.

To: Sam, Marnie and Henry

Also by Harry Dunn

He who fears death cannot enjoy life.
Spanish proverb

Chapter One

The car had just pulled in and parked when it happened. The body landed on the roof with such force that the female driver died instantly. The remains of the man lay face upwards, spread-eagled and naked on the crumpled metal above her. The explosion of sound stopped passers-by in their tracks and as the scene of horror slowly registered with them, the screaming began.

A passing police car cut across oncoming traffic switching on its blue lights before parking next to the scene. A young female police officer jumped out while shouting into her radio and ran towards the carnage. She could see the faller's head lying at an odd angle but felt for a pulse anyway. There was nothing. As she backed away, she found it impossible to miss the victim's open mouth still frozen as if in a silent scream. Two passers-by arrived and began wrenching at the driver's door but the crushed roof had jammed it shut. The two helpers then managed to ease the back door open about two inches and the police officer used her baton to force it out a little further. At last she stuck her head inside the vehicle. The sight before her was one of a blonde-haired woman who appeared lifeless from massive head and neck injuries. The PC checked for a pulse but there wasn't one. A red handbag lay on the passenger seat with its contents strewn over the floor.

As the officer backed out of the car, she heard the sound of approaching sirens and instinctively looked up. Out of the corner of her eye, she saw a sudden movement. It was a slatted blind flapping from an open window high up in the Hotel Majestic.

The emergency vehicles arrived with the scream of sirens and within minutes a green privacy tarpaulin had been erected around the car. The police officer felt sure that dozens of iPhones would have already captured the grisly end, but not the beginning.

Chapter Two

The days had been long and the nights even longer but Jack had struck gold for his last client. Literally. He didn't like being involved in divorce cases but this one had been different. When over £250,000 of jewellery had gone missing it gave the investigation an interesting angle and the fee on offer had been too tempting to refuse.

His thoughts drifted back to his last case as he crawled through west London traffic to his apartment in Maida Vale. As the early evening light faded, he found a residents' parking space nearby and walked back to his home in Elgin Avenue. He closed his door and made his way across to his small drinks cabinet and poured himself a Macallan before sitting down. Swirling it in the tumbler he smiled as he recalled the moment he'd found the gems. They were buried in a bag of wood bark in the husband's shed. The man's wife had told him he hated gardening and when Jack rummaged inside, he'd found the jewellery hidden in a plastic bag near the bottom. The man had successfully pleaded later in court that he'd placed the gems in the bag for security after their safe jammed. Nobody had been hurt except for feelings and bank balances after the divorce and Jack's fee would keep him afloat for three or even four months. He sipped the whisky and wished all his cases would be as straight forward and rewarding.

He'd nodded off and it took him a few moments to recognise the sudden noise as his phone rang. He picked up his mobile and at first, he thought he'd missed the caller. Then a female voice said, 'Mr Barclay?'

'Yes, this is Jack Barclay.'

'My name is Eva Long and I wondered if I could make an appointment to come and see you?' The voice was hesitant and he sensed nervousness.

'Of course you can. Do you know where my office is?'

'Yes, I know it. Would tomorrow morning be alright?'

'That would be fine. Shall we say 11am?'

'That would suit me.'

'Can I ask the reason for your call?'

'My sister died, Mr Barclay. They say it was an accident but...' Her voice faltered before she added, 'I need some answers.'

Chapter Three

The chaotic scenes at Hotel Majestic were not helped by Angelo the duty manager who seemed more concerned about his job than the two mangled bodies lying outside the main entrance to his prestigious hotel.

'My God, why has this happened?'

Police were everywhere, preventing people from leaving the hotel, and the lobby was becoming noisy with disgruntled customers.

'Come on, I need to be back at work,' a suited businessman whined.

More voices joined in as a uniformed police sergeant stood guard at the main entrance.

'Everyone will be interviewed,' said a young female detective, trying to be heard above the chatter. 'Please stay calm and we can get going in a couple of minutes. Be ready to show identification when asked.' A groan went round the lobby as three CSIs in white crime scene suits carrying metal cases eased their way through the crowd towards the lifts.

In contrast, outside there was an unusual silence. The road had been sealed off and figures clad in various uniforms could be seen going in behind the screens. A large patio-type umbrella had been erected above the side screens to stop people in the nearby buildings videoing the horror on their smart phones. As the Majestic's patrons began filtering out onto the pavement, they were ushered away from the scene.

A dark-grey windowless van reversed up the street and shortly after, the first of the two bodies was removed. By 4pm a tarpaulin had been draped and tied over the crushed vehicle before it was winched onto a low-loader. By 6.30 the screens were removed and the road re-opened to traffic. To anyone passing here now, there was nothing to suggest anything unusual had gone on today.

Chapter Four

Jack was typing up an invoice for a recent job involving a lost dog that had eventually been returned to its celebrity owner by a spurned lover. He'd only needed one close-up photograph to provide proof. The knock on his door came at 11am precisely. 'It's open,' he called.

Eva Long had shoulder-length auburn hair and looked to be in her thirties. Jack rose from behind his desk, stretching out his hand.

'Please sit down,' he said indicating the only other chair in the office.

Eva sat, discreetly crossing her long legs as she placed her tan shoulder bag on the thinly-carpeted floor.

'Can I offer you a tea or a coffee?'

'A glass of water would be fine, thank you.'

Jack went to the fridge and poured a small bottle of water into two glasses. As he turned back towards his visitor he noticed her watching him.

After taking a small sip of water, Eva leaned forward and placed the glass on the desk. 'I found your name online, Mr. Barclay. I know nothing about private detectives except what I've read. Some of it is good, some a bit scary.'

'Well, I hope you don't find me scary, and please call me Jack.'

'Okay, and please call me Eva.'

She seemed to relax a little and sank back in the upholstered chair. After taking a few breaths as if to steady herself, she looked straight at Jack and said, 'Something awful has happened and I need your help to find out why.'

Jack opened his notebook and took a pen from his jacket pocket. 'I hope I can help you.'

Eva's eyes brimmed with tears and she glanced down. 'My twin sister Susan has died in horrific circumstances. I don't think it was an accident, but everyone else thinks it was. I want to get to the bottom of it. I also want to know who did it.'

'Okay, Eva, from the beginning. Tell me everything.'

'Susan lived in two places, Spain and London, splitting her time between each. Although we didn't see each other as often as we would have liked, we spoke on the phone or texted. Sometimes she would visit me at my home in Clapham. Two weeks ago, she was driving through Kensington and pulled into the side of the road when a man fell from the top floor of a hotel and crashed onto her roof. The weird thing is, he was naked. They both died and I think it was instantaneous in both cases.' She paused to collect herself before speaking. 'I still can't believe she's gone.'

He'd seen it many times and he knew that no one was ever prepared for the loss of a loved one.

Eva composed herself and carried on. 'I had some concerns about her after she said her life in Spain had become very complicated. She didn't go into detail but I began to worry. Maybe it was all connected.'

'What do you mean?'

'We usually told each other everything about what was going on in our lives but she became secretive. I just thought that something wasn't right.'

Jack scribbled a note then asked, 'Were you told why she pulled over that day?'

'According to the police, a passer-by said a guy in a high-vis jacket stepped out from the pavement and flagged her into the side of the road. But they never found him and there's no CCTV of that happening. But why else would she have pulled in at the precise moment someone was jumping out of a window above her?'

'Do we know he jumped?'

'Oh, God, everyone assumed he was out of it or something.'

'Never assume anything, Eva. We haven't even started yet.'

Jack stayed silent for a moment and then said, 'I remember seeing this on the news. It seemed weird at the time but it's gone quiet since. I'm prepared to try and help but I'll need a lot of information about your sister. I'll need to know everything you know, even things you may not wish to talk about.' He looked at her and thought she nearly smiled.

'Thank you. I've hardly slept since it happened and, well, it's good to have someone helping me. What are your charges?'

'I take a fee up front to cover initial costs and then bill on a regular basis. We can come to some suitable arrangement. If a client doesn't pay along the way then I stop. That doesn't happen often I'm pleased to say. Sound okay to you?'

'Yes, thank you.'

'Now, tell me about Susan.'

Eva smiled. 'She was the adventurous type, you know. Used to get me into trouble when we were young. She always seemed to have something exciting going on in her life and she was good to be with. Men and women loved her company because she was fun. She liked the good things in life and after one holiday in Spain many years ago, she became so hooked on Marbella she finished up moving there.' She paused and took a deep breath. 'We lost our mum and dad a few years back so there was only the two of us.'

Jack was making notes. 'Did she live in Marbella?'

'No in Malaga. She'd made friends there and property was cheaper, but she spent a lot of time around Marbella and Puerto Banús. She was in the beauty business and she had a lot of wealthy customers living around there.'

'Could you give me the address of her home in Malaga?'

Eva picked up her phone and scrolled before handing it to him. The district where Susan lived meant nothing to him but he wrote down the details and handed the phone back.

'Could you be a bit more specific about her business?' he asked.

'It was called Beach Babe and she supplied luxury products to beauty salons and hairdressers along the coast. At first, she had her own salon in Marbella and built up quite a reputation for therapies. Business boomed, but in the end she said it just became hard work and she began concentrating on supplying the other beauty outlets. The profit margins were small but she soon began cutting out the wholesalers in the Costa Del Sol and buying direct from suppliers in London.'

Jack looked up. 'That seems an odd way to make more profit. What was she buying?'

'I don't know enough about it but I think she began collecting beauty products herself. She usually drove. We used to meet in London when she was on a buying trip. Business with pleasure thrown in. She often laughed and said I was tax deductible.'

Jack raised his hand to indicate a pause. 'That's a long journey to make. How often did she do it?'

'Well, I don't know if she contacted me each time but I saw her around five times each year. I just put it down to her love of fast cars. She said she enjoyed the freedom and usually broke her journey once in Spain and once in France.'

'And where did she stay in London?'

'She stayed with me in Clapham but sometimes she said she was staying with a friend. She also found a small hotel in Chiswick where she liked to stay. I asked her why but she just avoided answering and I sometimes thought she could be with a boyfriend. She always insisted on taking me out for a slap-up meal and she invited me to parties, but I usually had to get to work the next day so didn't often go.'

Eva pressed her palms to her eyes and Jack stayed silent as she began composing herself. 'I'm sorry,' she said. 'I still can't believe all this. I can't bear to think I'll never see her again. I miss her so much.'

'I know these questions are difficult for you but I have to ask them. Can I get you anything?'

'No, it's okay. Thank you. Am I being any help to you?'

'Oh yes, I'm getting a picture. I'll probably have more questions but not necessarily today. A couple of final things, though. Can you give me the dates when she travelled to London in the last year? I also need her full name. The one on her passport.'

'Susan Marie Long. I'll have to check my diary for the dates she visited me.'

'Did she use social media at all?'

'No, she seemed reluctant to share information about herself. She had a website for her beauty products a couple of years ago, but it doesn't seem to be active anymore. I assume she'd built up enough contacts and didn't need to get her name out there.'

'Okay, I need a recent photo of her.'

Eva picked up her phone again. 'I've got one here. It was taken on her last visit to London and you'll see we're quite alike, but not identical. I'll send it to you now.' She traced her finger across the photo on the screen, fresh tears filling her eyes as she pressed the send button.

'I think that's enough for now,' Jack said gently. 'I'll start making a few enquiries, but maybe we could talk again soon. If you think of things that could be useful just jot them down for me. I'll call you tomorrow around eleven and we can arrange another meeting.

I know how difficult this is for you, Eva and I'm so sorry for your loss.'

Eva nodded and rose from her chair. 'Thank you, Jack. I feel better for having talked about it. We'll speak tomorrow.'

Jack watched her as she walked towards the door. She paused and turned around to smile at him before leaving.

Chapter Five

It was 9pm in Malaga and still 28C. Every restaurant was rammed with tourists and the odd local. Life was good. In a small back office just off Calle Velarde, two men sat at an antique cherry-wood table. Each had a brandy glass in front of him and a half-full bottle of Solera Gran Reserva stood in front of the host.

'The London operation went to plan and the problem has gone away. Two birds were killed with one stone, as they say.'

The words were spoken by a middle-aged man as he finished sipping his second brandy. Although in his late thirties, Vicente Perez had kept himself in good shape and was well known around the tourist night clubs in the city. Women seemed to go for his chiselled good looks, and the way he threw his money around only made him more attractive. He swept his right hand through his thick black hair then pulled a Marlborough Red out of a packet. Passing the pack across the table towards his boss, he lit up and inhaled deeply.

Rico nodded and took a slug of his drink before sneering, 'They won't be missed, but we have a package to move to London in the next twenty-four hours so we need a driver. Who can do it?'

Vicente grunted. 'I can fix that. I need to make a couple of calls though.'

'Do what you need to do and make it work.'

'Okay. It'll probably be Salvador.'

'There'll be a kilo of fentanyl,' Rico said. 'How many runs has he done? New drivers make me nervous.'

Vicente heard the aggression in his voice. 'Only one, but he's cool. He'll be fine.' Sensing Rico's anger he quickly picked up his mobile to make a call. He listened for a couple of minutes and turned to Ricardo when the conversation ended. 'The car will be prepared tonight and it'll be ready for collection at noon tomorrow. I'll make sure all the usual rules will apply. Salvador will be fully briefed for the border checks. He shouldn't have any problems. He's on a business trip and will be dressed smart. Two nights in London for appearances then straight back. I'll keep you briefed throughout.'

'Do that and don't fuck up.' Rico finished his drink in one gulp and slammed the empty glass onto the table before pushing back his chair and making for the door.

As soon as he'd left, Vicente exhaled before picking up his mobile. 'Juan, it's Vicente.'

'What's up?'

'I've just had a visit from Rico and he wasn't too happy about Salvador as the driver, but I told him he'd done a run before, although never with fentanyl. Where are you going to put it?'

'A half inside each wing mirror. I'll confirm everything first thing in the morning.'

'Whatever,' the voice grunted.

Vicente killed the call. He lit another cigarette and checked his watch. It would be four in the afternoon in London. His phone had enough juice left for one more call.

In Shoreditch the voice said 'Hello' within two rings.

Vicente greeted him with, 'Hola, Frank.' Although there was no one else in the office, he lowered his voice. 'Any comeback from Susan's death?'

'Nothing yet. The pathology report will show the faller had taken cocaine before he went out the window. It'll look like wrong place, wrong time.'

'I hope so,' Vicente said. 'There's a shipment leaving tomorrow, so should be with you on Friday. Usual route, different driver. He's called Salvador. After all the problems with Susan, this shipment is even more important, Frank. I'll speak to you in the morning and give you more details.'

Vicente ended the call and leaned back in his chair. His thoughts turned to the last week that had ended so disastrously. He knew he had to up his game. The mass of logistics he had to put in place throughout the organisation to make Susan's death appear a random accident seemed to account for nothing with Rico. If Salvador was to be the courier, a lot was riding on him to deliver safely and re-build Vicente's reputation. He decided to visit Juan first thing in the morning and check all the preparations for himself.

He left his office and walked out into the stifling night air. It was 11 o'clock. With no Susan to visit in her welcoming villa in Los Montes, it was time to hit the clubs. As he walked to his car, he thought of the times he'd visited Susan after dark. When the nights were hot he'd often find her by the pool at the rear of the villa, sometimes naked and usually with a gin and tonic in her hand. He would pour himself a Soberano and strip off before joining her. It never took long before they retreated to the sofa in the covered patio and began to enjoy each other's bodies. Maybe it was the heat, maybe it was the booze, but they both knew what they liked and the sex had always been good. Glistening with sweat after their lovemaking, he loved their ritual: a shower by the pool before a dip to cool off. Vicente could have stared at her wonderful body forever and he usually led her back to the sofa after a couple more drinks. Susan didn't mind him turning up unannounced. She seemed to like surprises and he knew the knowledge of what was about to happen only heightened her excitement.

As he drove past groups of girls making their way to the late-night clubs, he pushed Susan out of his mind. He'd have a good time at his pool in a few hours' time. It would be business as usual.

Chapter Six

Jack made his way home to his apartment. Traffic seemed worse tonight, if that was possible. Eventually, he found a residents' parking space for his ageing black SAAB 900 and began to walk back towards Elgin Avenue. As he strolled past beautiful white stucco period houses, he thought of his meeting with Eva. There was no doubt her suspicions were justified. He made a mental note to find out more about the man in the high-vis jacket. It was his action that caused her death. Would the guy have fallen onto Susan's car if she hadn't pulled in? Would he have fallen at all? Jack arrived at his apartment block and climbed the stairs. The post was lying behind the door but there was nothing of interest and he binned the lot in the kitchen.

He checked his landline for messages but there had been no calls. Kicking off his shoes, he went to the drinks cabinet and poured himself a Macallan before picking up his laptop and dropping into his armchair. Googling 'Beach Babe' he was offered a blizzard of bikini-clad women. Adding Marbella to his search didn't change things much. He moved onto 'Susan Long' but nothing relevant came up. From the absence of any information, Jack knew it was likely that data had been removed. The scene of death was the only connection he had.

Lying in bed later, the thoughts began to tumble through his mind. He wondered why Susan always drove to London. It was a hell of a long journey. Why not fly and have products shipped back to Malaga? How did Eva know so little about her sister? It just didn't add up. He decided to visit the Hotel Majestic in the morning.

***

The hotel's plaque said it had four stars. It was 9.00am and taxis were pulling up for departing guests. Jack stood in a doorway across the road and watched. Traffic was heavy and progress for the weary drivers at this time in the morning was slow. There were two traffic lanes going east and two lanes going west, but east into the city was still at a crawl. A small lay-by in front of the hotel could accommodate three vehicles at the most and Jack knew from the descriptions he'd had that this is where Susan had been directed by the man in the high-vis jacket. Looking up, he saw a boarded-up window on the top floor of the Majestic, directly above the lay-by.

He waited a little longer and let his eyes wander either side of the hotel entrance. To the right he saw a news vendor at his stand about fifty yards from the entrance to the hotel. To the left was a sandwich bar. Using the crossing, he made his way to the hotel and walked into the lobby. It seemed very welcoming without being grand. A high ceiling gave a certain air of importance and there was plenty of space for all the comings and goings. Jack made his way to an armchair at the side of the foyer and sat down. As he watched, he noted all the usual activities of a well-run hotel. Everything was running smoothly as far as he could tell. All the front of house staff appeared young with the exception of one slightly stooped, grey-haired luggage porter who looked as if he'd seen it all before.

As Jack got up to leave, he walked close to him and looked at his name badge. Norman. Everyone was busy and Jack walked on and out through the revolving door to the street, turning left. He slowed as he approached the newspaper seller and waited until the stand was free of customers. The vendor looked to be in his sixties with a thin but friendly face. He had a flat cap on his head and wore a dark, heavy coat. When Jack approached, the old man looked up as if he knew Jack was not a passing customer. 'You look like a copper.'

'Used to be a long time ago, but not now. Is it that obvious?'

'No, just instinct. What are you after?'

'Were you here on the day the man fell out of the window of the Majestic?'

'Yes, I was here. Didn't see anything much though.'

Jack pulled a ten-pound note from his pocket and palmed it to him. The old man smiled, showing nicotine-stained teeth.

'It was a bad day. Bodies everywhere. Cost me a lot of business when they closed the road off.'

Jack asked, 'Did you see anything unusual before the man fell?'

'Yeah. A guy with a bright yellow jacket appeared from nowhere and walked out into the traffic. He was on his phone all the time. I watched him because of the noise of horns from the cars.'

'What happened next?'

'He stuck his arm up and waved a car to the side of the road.'

'In front of the hotel?'

'Yes, and that's when the bloke landed on the car.'

'What happened to the man in the yellow jacket?'

'He vanished. Don't know where he went.'

'Could you describe him?'

'A bit. Hang on.' He served a customer with a copy of The Times and threw the coins in a tin. He looked back at Jack and asked, 'Where were we?'

'A description of the yellow jacket man.'

'He looked young. A bit skinny. Couldn't see his face much as his collar was turned up. Short dark hair. He seemed to know who he was looking for.'

Jack stood back as a customer bought a magazine then he stepped forward again.

'That's all I know, mister.'

'You've been very helpful. One last thing, did the man scream as he fell?'

'Nope. Not a sound until he hit the car.'

Jack dug into his pocket and took out another ten-pound note. 'Thank you for your time.'

'No problem.'

Turning round, Jack walked back towards the Majestic and looked up as he approached it. He couldn't see any CCTV cameras but that didn't mean there weren't any. Going through the revolving doors of the hotel, he chose a seat by the window and watched the lobby area again. By ten o'clock things had quietened down and as Norman walked by, Jack said, 'Excuse me.'

Norman stopped. 'Yes, sir.'

Jack stood up. 'I'm looking for a bit of help from you. It's about the day the woman was killed in the car outside.'

'I'm sorry but I can't help you. I wasn't here that day.' The porter turned round and started to walk away.

Jack raised his voice slightly and said, 'She could have been murdered.'

Norman stopped and then walked back. 'It was an accident, wasn't it?'

'Maybe, maybe not. She was deliberately flagged into the side of the road before being crushed to death. Her sister has asked me for help. I'm a private investigator.'

The man's shoulders sagged and he held up his hands. Lowering his voice, he said, 'I'll tell you what I know, but not here. I finish my shift in an hour. I go to the Kings Arms round the corner. Meet me in there.'

***

The pub was empty except for a lone drinker at the bar. Jack asked the young dark-haired barmaid for a pint of beer and took a seat near the window but in sight of the door. Norman came in about ten minutes later. He'd changed into a dark jacket and trousers. He looked around, spotted Jack and headed for the bar. Jack beat him to it and said, 'This is on me.'

'Okay, just a bottle of pale ale.'

They sat by the window and as Norman placed his glass on the table he said, 'What did you say your name was?'

Jack fished out his card and passed it to him. 'My name is Jack Barclay and I'm a private detective and I pay good money for information. I'll be grateful for any help you can give me, especially anything about the guy who fell.' Giving Norman a second to digest this he asked, 'Had you seen him in the hotel before that morning?'

'No never. I shouldn't really be talking to you because the manager has told us not to say anything about what happened.'

Jack sipped his beer and asked, 'Why do you think that is?'

'I don't know.' Norman glanced around. 'I think the manager is trying to get rid of me because of my age, but what happened shouldn't be covered up and I could do with a few extra quid. I can't tell you too much, but I do know the young guy who died wasn't down as being a guest at all. He was just visiting. God knows what happened up there. We've got cameras in some of the corridors and the police have taken all the video with them. That's about all I know.'

'What do you think about it all, Norman?'

'Well, it was a heavy morning. We had groups from Australia and America on a big European tour.' He took a swig of his beer. 'Trip of a lifetime they all said, but they were tired and the check-out was slow. There were people everywhere and lots of big cases to move. Truth is, anyone could've come and gone that morning.' Norman leaned in towards Jack and said quietly, 'He fell naked and Irene the maid said the bed clothes were rumpled but the bed hadn't been slept in. I wonder if it was some sex game gone wrong.'

Jack looked up and knew he'd just heard the news that changed everything. He brought out his wallet, took three twenties out and folded them. 'Have another drink on me. You can be sure this conversation never took place. If you hear anything more give me a call.'

Norman grabbed the notes before pushing them quickly into the top pocket of his jacket. 'Thank you. I can certainly use the money right now. I'll get in touch if I hear anything else, Mr Barclay.'

Jack emptied his glass and rose. 'I appreciate your help.'

Chapter Seven

Vicente was feeling the effects of his night out. He'd picked up a young female tourist at 'Bianca's' and they'd had little sleep after returning to his place at 1am. By the time he woke at 7am the black satin sheets were in a heap at the side of the king size bed. After pouring her a glass of orange juice, he ordered a taxi for the girl and promised he'd see her again in two nights' time at the club. She told him that it would be her last night before going home and she'd be with her two friends. She scowled at him when he grinned and said, 'You can all come back.'

Traffic was already becoming heavier as he made his way across the city to the Guadalhorce industrial area. Juan's garage was a nondescript breeze block building with shutters in front of the windows. As Vicente pulled up across the road he saw the heavy padlocks on the double gates. Juan arrived at 8.30 to open up for the day. As Vicente drove his white BMW through the open gates, he saw a black Audi tucked inside the building.

Juan walked up to the driver's door. 'Checking up on me, eh!'

Vicente just laughed and retorted, 'Got to get this one right, Juan. I need to see you hide the packages.' Juan recoiled and he realised his breath must still reek of alcohol.

They walked inside and Juan switched on the overhead florescent strip lights before closing the garage doors and locking them. Vicente blinked sharply as the garage was bathed in light and he saw Juan fixing him with a cold stare. Vicente walked round the car and noticed how immaculate it looked both outside and in. He could smell the aroma of fresh polish that had been used, then he caught his reflection in the driver's window. 'God, I look like shit,' he exclaimed.

Juan just rolled his eyes, grinned and said, 'You want to try getting some sleep when you go to bed.'

Vicente turned back to the car and asked, 'So, where you going to stash the stuff?'

'Like I said, in the wing mirrors. There are no motors inside them now.' Juan took a tiny screwdriver and prised open the driver's wing mirror casing. Turning to Vicente he pointed to the cavity. I've coated the inside with a mix of tungsten and carbon paper. The dogs won't smell a thing if they go round the car.'

Vicente nodded. 'That's good. Are you ready with the packages?'

'Yeah, all set.' Juan went to the back of the garage and disappeared through a wooden door that had photographs of the Barcelona footballers pinned on it. He was back in a couple of minutes and Vicente watched as he placed two bags on a side table. Two bags of fentanyl, enough to kill thousands. Juan had a look of concentration on his face as he picked one of the bags up and eased into the cavity of the driver's mirror. He pressed it in tightly and replaced the casing before rubbing the outside of the mirrors to clean off any prints. Vicente was impressed as he examined Juan's handiwork and watched as he walked round the car to the other mirror. The whole operation took twenty minutes and Vicente checked both mirrors again before satisfying himself that the car looked absolutely normal.

'Happy?' Juan asked.

'Yeah, looks good.'

Juan started to pack his tools away and, without looking up, asked, 'What happened to Susan? I thought she was the best?'

Vicente hesitated before answering. 'She blew her cover. Too many drinks one night in London and she said something she shouldn't have. We had no choice. I don't want to talk about it.'

Juan shrugged. 'When is Salvador coming for the car?'

'I'm going to brief him this morning. You should have the car back by next Monday. It could be late so you'll have to stick around.'

Juan just nodded. 'Fine.'

Vicente drove back towards the city and parked near El Barco. He needed coffee and a good breakfast and this was his favourite place. It was busy with locals and he chose a table near the back. The air was already stifling, but he was out of earshot of other customers. He took out his phone and tapped on a contact number. The voice only said 'Hello' but to Vicente it was unmistakeable.

'Rico, we're ready to go today. It's well hidden and the driver is confirmed as Salvador. He goes this afternoon.'

'You don't need to say any more. It had better be the best run. No mistakes.'

Vicente winced. 'Will do.' He heard the call being cut just as the waitress arrived with his *café con leche* and *ensaimadas*. He felt like shit and was glad Rico hadn't wanted to see him today. His hand trembled slightly as he reached out for his coffee. *'Muchas gracias.'*

The girl smiled. *'De nada.'*

His next call would be to Frank in London, but first he had to eat something. *God, I must cut down on the booze.*

Chapter Eight

Jack left the Kings Arms and walked back to take a last look at the outside of the hotel from the other side of the road. He gazed up and scanned the layout of the front of the hotel. He was fairly sure that someone who literally fell out of a high window would land on the pavement. To land on a car parked at the side of the road would need a little propulsion. The man in the high-vis jacket must have played a key role, but thinking about Norman's information on the state of the room made him sure that Susan had been murdered. He needed to speak to Eva and he knew she wouldn't like his questions.

Standing in a doorway, he pulled out his phone and dialled her number.

She picked up immediately.

'I've found out a few things, but we need to meet,' Jack told her.

He heard an intake of breath. 'Just name the place and time.'

'Is tomorrow morning any good? How about my office at 10 o'clock?'

'Yes, that's fine.'

'I'll see you then.' Jack closed the call and sat back in his chair. *I need to know what she knows.*

***

Eva knocked on Jack's door at 10am precisely. He was making coffee and asked her if she'd like a cup.

'Yes, thank you. No sugar.' She was wearing a light-green dress and nude-coloured high heels.

'Have a seat, Eva. I'll be right with you.'

Since last night he had been wondering how to break the news to her and as he sat down he was still none the wiser. He couldn't be positive about Susan being murdered, but everything pointed that way.

'I take it you've made some headway but I think it's going to be bad news, Jack.'

'Yes, it is. You had some thoughts yourself about your sister's death and I believe you were right to be suspicious. There's no easy way to say this. I've visited the spot where Susan died and from the conversations I've had with various people I'm afraid to say I think it was unlikely to be accidental.' He stopped talking as Eva's head dropped.

She covered her face with her hands, sitting quietly for a few moments.

'I'm sorry,' Jack continued, 'but that's the way it seems right now.'

Eva looked up at him. 'I was always worried about what Susan was up to in the last few months. It's what she didn't say to me as much as what she did. Sometimes I asked her things, but she just wriggled out of answering me straight.'

Jack sipped his coffee and leaned forward. 'What did you think Susan was involved in?'

'I don't know. She began dodging questions about her business and wouldn't tell me anything. When she started out you couldn't stop her talking. The business was her life and she was loving Spain. I used to visit her but then she stopped inviting me. I knew she was hiding things from me. Sisters know. Especially twins.'

'Did you meet any of her friends in Malaga?'

'She seemed to know a lot of ex-pats in the area and when I was there she'd throw parties at her villa. They all seemed a pleasant bunch. I don't think she knew any of them that well actually. I think she was trying to promote her business.'

'Did your sister have a boyfriend?'

'I saw a text message the last time I was out there.' She paused. 'I would say they were close.'

'Why?'

'It was late one night and we'd stayed in and had drinks by the pool. Susan had gone inside and her phone bleeped. I thought it was mine because they were the same colour, so I picked it up to

28

check the message. It was from someone called Vicente and he said he was coming round to see her. It said: Necesito sexo. I suppose that's why I remember him. Susan checked her phone when she came back out and I saw her send a message. The guy never appeared.'

Jack wrote down the name. 'When Susan made her trips to London did she contact you as soon as she arrived?'

'She always had lots of beauty stuff in the car so I think she'd finished any buying before meeting me.'

'Driving all the way to London to buy beauty products. Does that make sense to you? I mean, she could just have ordered them online and had them shipped to Malaga.'

'I often wondered about that. She said she didn't like flying and it was a chance to see friends and me.' Eva smiled wistfully. 'And she enjoyed driving fast cars.'

'Do you know where she bought her beauty stuff?'

'She mentioned some wholesale place in Walthamstow, but I never took much notice.'

'On the day she died do you know where Susan was going?'

'We'd spoken on the phone and she said she had to meet someone in Paddington but she didn't go into detail. I assumed it was to do with her work.' She hesitated before saying, 'Something's been bothering me and I can't really can't get my head round it.'

Jack said, 'Ask away.'

'If Susan was murdered and the guy in the Majestic was thrown out of the window, how did they know Susan would be underneath in her car?'

'The timing was down to the guy in the high-vis jacket. He co-ordinated it. After he signalled her to pull into the side, he simply called up to the room on his phone. He then stood in the road in front of the car so Susan couldn't move. She would have been in the exact position to align her car roof below the window. The guy in the yellow jacket disappeared immediately. His job was done and he didn't want to be filmed when the smart phones came out.'

Eva flinched as she listened and said, 'Why on earth would anyone want to do that to Susan? She was a great person!

Everyone thought so.' Shaking her head, she whispered, 'I can't believe this.'

'We haven't really started yet but it looks likely she had another life you didn't know about. What I do need to do is visit her home in Malaga. Have the police returned any of her possessions to you yet?'

'No, but I'm expecting a call from them tomorrow.'

'When you get the contents of her bag back, I'd like to look through them. It's likely the police might also want to make their own checks on her Malaga villa, but it doesn't stop us doing it too.'

'Us?'

'I think you should be present and there will be a lot of legal stuff you'll need to sort out. Maybe bills to pay. I'll stay at a local hotel and you may want to stay at Susan's place. We should move quickly. Can you get away for a few days?'

'My company has been very understanding. It won't be a problem but I don't want to stay on my own at Susan's villa. It wouldn't feel right and it would be scary.'

'I understand. Let's try for a flight on Thursday. That gives me two days to make flight and hotel arrangements. I'll let you know the times.'

'How many nights should I pack for?'

'I'd say three for you but I'll make the tickets flexible. I may have to stay on longer depending on what I find. Don't mention the trip to anyone. Just say you're out of town for a few days.'

'It's going to be a difficult journey for me and I'm glad you'll be there.'

She tried to smile and Jack knew how hard this was for her. 'I'll be doing some digging here before we set off,' he told her, 'but I'll keep in touch. If you think of anything else just call me.'

She looked him in the eye and said, 'I will and I'll wait to hear from you. I've never been involved with anything like this before, Jack. I'm quite scared now.'

Jack watched her get up from the chair and smooth down her dress before she turned for the door.

***

Once Eva had left, Jack sat back and reflected on what they had. He was short on leads and knew most of the answers probably lay in leg work when he arrived in Malaga. He Googled Susan's Malaga address and got nothing. Linking her address with Beach Babe drew a blank. He was surprised. A once successful businesswoman, beautiful and popular, with many friends, had been erased from the internet. Never existed. He drank the last of his coffee and switched off his laptop, knowing he was going to Malaga with precious little to go on. The only name he had was Vicente.

Chapter Nine

Salvador started up the Audi 6 and drove out of Juan's garage calling out of the open driver's window. 'See you back here Monday.' They all knew this was the biggest run. The fentanyl Salvador was carrying had a massive street value when cut with low-grade heroin or cocaine.

Vicente lit a Marlboro and inhaled deeply as he looked up and exhaled smoke through his mouth and nose. *Christ let him get him through.* He went outside and phoned Rico. 'On its way.'

Rico's voice still had the traces of his family's Moroccan roots and Vicente had to listen carefully to make sure he understood everything. 'Okay, keep in touch with me. No fuck ups.'

Vicente heard a click as the call was ended and he sighed with relief. He knew Rico would be funding this shipment and failure wasn't an option. He scrolled down his contacts list and called Frank in London. 'He's just left.'

'I'll be waiting.'

Vicente walked back into the garage and nodded to Juan. 'I'll be in touch.' He climbed into his car and weaved his way out of the industrial estate.

***

Jack met Eva at Terminal Five at Heathrow for their Iberia flight to Malaga. As they waited in line to pass through security he asked, 'Have you spoken to the police again about Susan?'

'Yes, they came to my flat last night. They were very sympathetic. I told them I was going to Susan's place in Malaga to pay some bills. They gave me the villa keys from her bag but I didn't mention you were going too.'

'Did they give you her mobile phone?'

'No, they're still processing information from it. Said they'd let me know when they were finished.'

'Did they tell you anything about the guy who fell?'

'They're awaiting the autopsy results. They couldn't give me a name but they were keeping an open mind. They asked me questions again about Susan, but as you know, I couldn't help them much. One thing they did say confused me. The car she was driving wasn't hers.'

Jack looked up quickly.

'They said it was owned by a company in Gibraltar. That's all they'd tell me.'

'Did Susan have any connections there?'

'I really don't know. It's a bit weird.'

'We will probably find out that weird becomes normal as we go on.' Jack stopped talking and looked at the departure board. 'That's us. Let's go.'

They landed in Malaga at 7pm. Jack had booked them into the Hotel Carmen and they checked in at 8.30.

In the lobby, Eva turned to Jack. 'I'm hungry. How about some dinner?'

'Sure. See you down here in twenty minutes.'

'Make it fifteen.'

They left the hotel and walked out into the hot September evening. Jack pointed to a restaurant after a short stroll.

Sabores Ancianos was busy, but they were led to a table and offered menus. Jack saw the strain on Eva's face as she looked around at the carefree diners in the restaurant and he realised how much she must be dreading the next few days.

'What would you like to drink?'

Her face brightened. 'I'd love a glass of Rioja because I'm going to have the roast lamb.'

Jack replied, 'Let's have a bottle because I'm going to have the same.'

As she sipped her wine she asked, 'I'm wondering why you are sitting here in Malaga with me, Jack? You must have some lucrative job offers come your way. Why me?'

Jack was unprepared for her question and remained silent for a few seconds. 'I like you and I want to help you. Simple as that. When I was in the police I had no choice in who I investigated. The hours were very unpredictable and the internal politics annoyed me. If I had my life to live over again I would do things differently and I wouldn't have joined the police. Spending all your time chasing bad boys is not good for a relationship. Villains don't work nine to five and it takes its toll.'

'Well, thank you for taking my case.' She raised her glass. 'I really appreciate it.'

He nodded and smiled. 'I want to find out who killed your sister.'

They stopped talking briefly when their meals arrived and as they ate, Jack noticed how relaxed Eva became as she talked about Spain and how much she enjoyed the culture and way of life.

After Jack paid the bill, they threaded their way around the tables and made for the door before walking slowly back to the Hotel Carmen. The warm night sounds of soft guitar music from a nearby bar and the intoxicating smells of jasmine filled the air and both became silent. Jack was already thinking about the next day.

As they approached the hotel he said, 'I have a hire car being delivered in the morning at 9.00. We need to be ready to go to Susan's home, so let's meet for breakfast at 7.30.'

Collecting their keys from reception, Jack turned and said, 'Goodnight, Eva. Try to sleep well.'

'I'll try.'

***

It was cloudless over Malaga next morning and at 7.30 the breakfast room was already busy. Jack found a small table on the outside terrace and placed his orange juice down. Eva joined him a couple of minutes later and although many of the guests around them were talking loudly, they didn't speak much as they ate.

'Sleep okay, Eva?'

'It was very hot and sometimes I'm a bit funny on my own in a strange bed.' She looked at Jack, a smile on her face.

He let out little laugh. 'Yeah, it was too hot for sleep.'

They talked about the day ahead and finished their breakfast.

'I'm going to wait outside for the hire car,' Jack told her. 'I'll see you out there when you're ready.'

Signing the hire car paperwork, Jack hoped he hadn't left some important little box un-ticked.

After the rental man had gone, he sat in the car to familiarise himself with the controls and then he put Susan's address into the sat nav and switched it to English. Eva appeared a few minutes later. She buckled herself in as Jack indicated right and waited before moving into the traffic.

The journey to the Los Montes district took them twenty minutes through the morning traffic and Eva hardly said a word on the way. The voice on the sat nav told Jack to turn right and they entered a narrow street lined with hedges of flowering purple and white bougainvillea.

Eva looked out of her window and said, 'The house is further up on the left.'

Jack had slowed right down when the voice said, 'Arriving at destination.'

Eva pointed her hand in front of Jack. 'That's Susan's right there.'

He pulled into the side and parked half-way on the pavement to allow traffic to pass. Switching off the engine he turned to Eva and asked, 'Are you okay?'

'I'm a bit wobbly, but I'll be fine.' She rummaged in her bag for the keys and stepped out of the car. A white-painted metal gate was unlocked and they closed it behind them before walking up the narrow path to the front door. Eva tried two keys before finding the correct one and the door swung open to reveal a darkened hallway.

Jack stepped in first and stayed close to the right-hand wall, indicating to Eva to stay behind him. They stopped as they approached the first internal door, aware of the repressive heat inside.

Pushing the door open, Jack looked into the main room and knew immediately the place had been expertly tossed. His eyes went to a dresser on the right side of the room and every drawer was open. It had been searched from the bottom up and clothes were strewn all over the floor. Paintings had been ripped from walls and the stuffing torn from upturned chairs was covering much of the floor. The flat-screen TV had been smashed open and lay in pieces. Jack knew every room in the house would have had similar treatment.

Eva followed him in and gasped. 'Oh, my God.'

Jack put a hand on her arm. 'I don't think there is anyone here now, but stay behind me, Eva.'

They moved into the kitchen to find cabinet doors open and utensils scattered over the floor. Contents of tins and jars lay over the kitchen tops and even light sockets had been pulled apart. They moved upstairs to a further scene of absolute mayhem. Nothing had been spared and not one of the rooms was habitable. Floorboards had been taken up and the remnants of mattresses lay everywhere. Every light fixture was hanging from ceilings. Jack poked his head into the family bathroom and the en-suite knowing full well what he would see and he wasn't surprised. More ripped-out chaos.

'Who's been here, Jack?'

'Professionals. This is to do with money and Susan must have been mixed up in something very big for this sort of attention.'

'Do you think they found what they were looking for?'

'Can't tell.'

Eva was shaking. 'Can we go outside? I've seen enough in here.'

The heat had built up in the short time they had been inside and Jack wished he'd brought a hat with him. Eva stayed in the shade as he began to walk around the pool to get an idea of the lay-out. Sun loungers were stacked at one end and the pool cover was in place to stop too many insects flying in for a last dip. He approached the housing cover with the humming filtration system and leaned against it looking back to the house. His eyes swept round the outside of the pool and he counted four stands each holding a large red life-saving ring. One at each of the four sides and for the size of the pool it looked a generous thought on someone's part. The one at the shallow end seemed new compared with the sun-bleached state of the others. He wandered over and un-hooked it, surprised at its weight. Moving round to the next one he lifted it and found it much lighter. He returned to the first one and turned it over to look at the reverse side. A break in the stitching caught his eye and he picked at it with his fingers. A small slit appeared and he eased it open and stuck his index finger inside. He immediately hit resistance and pulled the two sides apart with both hands. He saw black rubberised wrapping and ran his nail along it. The first banknote he knew to be a 500-euro one just by the colour. Pulling more of the exterior apart he found himself looking at a fortune. The ring was stuffed to capacity with 500-euro notes. He walked back out of the heat into the house and set the ring down on the coffee table.

Eva followed him in and stared at the pile of notes. 'What on earth is that?'

'Probably half a million euros.'

'My God, Jack, how did you know where to find that?'

'I didn't. I just spotted something odd by the pool. You know what this sort of money means, don't you?'

'No. I haven't a clue.'

'Your sister was involved with drugs. Nothing else on the planet generates this sort of cash.'

'Is that why she died?'

'Probably.'

'So, why is it still here?'

'Whoever ripped Susan's house apart couldn't find it. There will be some desperate people searching for this money.'

'What do we do now?'

'I'll phone the police in Malaga and tell them what we know. This is a crime scene now. Probably a million-euro crime scene.'

Jack picked up his phone and Googled the number for Malaga police. He rang and asked to speak with the senior detective on duty. After what he was about to tell them, he knew they'd be here soon.

'We'll have to wait here, Eva. It's going to be a long day.'

'Well, you've found something big and I'll just wait with you.'

As he looked through the open patio doors at the pool area, he realised how clever the hiding place was. No one takes any notice of the rings round the side unless they're drowning.

***

Jack showed the ring with all the money to Ramon Valez, the Spanish detective inspector, and explained how he'd found it. The inspector's English was almost perfect, and Jack explained that he was a private investigator and Eva was his client. He gave him details on Susan and how she had died in a London street two weeks earlier.

'I don't know why all this money was here,' Jack said, 'and I don't know why the house has been trashed, but I would guess it's drug money. It must have been what they were after.'

The detective nodded in agreement. 'We know about the death in London and we are making enquiries about the car the deceased was driving. I appreciate your help but you must know this is a police matter. We'll just take some of your details and where you are staying. We'll need to see you again and take your prints for elimination. I'm very sorry for your loss, Miss Long. As soon as we've finished our forensic investigation here you are free to return home.'

Eva nodded and sighed. 'Thank you. I didn't think things could get much worse, but it's been another bad day for me.'

Chapter Ten

Salvador was making good progress and by dusk he was within striking distance of Madrid. He felt alert and decided to drive on. He loved the car, but kept to the speed limit because his sat nav warned him of the speed cameras. His inability to adjust the wing mirrors told him where the drugs were hidden and he smiled to himself as he travelled north. As the light began to fade he kept going. He loved the night.

Lights ahead told him there was a filling station, which was a relief because he needed diesel and something to eat. He pulled in and brought the fuel level up to full before locking the car.

Inside the station he chose a pizza with chorizo and asked the guy to heat it in the microwave for him. He kept looking out to the car but it seemed to be a quiet night and no one else had driven in. He paid for his fuel and pizza in cash and went back into the evening heat. Driving slowly towards the far corner of the parking area he pulled up behind a truck with UK plates. The cab curtains were drawn.

Feeling under his seat, he brought out a torch and quietly opened his door. He dropped to the ground, put on a pair of cotton gloves and shone the light under the front of his car. The tracking device was attached to the metal wall of the wheel well and he gently eased it off by twisting it 180 degrees. He stood up and pulled out his mobile phone as he approached the rear of the truck. Using duct tape, he joined the tracker and phone together and bent down to move under the tail of the lorry. Choosing his spot, he taped both devices tightly to a strut under the trailer. He crawled from under the trailer, climbed back into his car and drove slowly towards the exit.

There was a toll booth ahead and he put his pizza down on the seat next to him. Choosing the cash lane, he paid the fee, drove through and carried on towards the junction for Madrid.

***

The pain in Eva's eyes was obvious to Jack after the day at her sister's villa. It was one tragedy after another and they were silent as they drove back to the Hotel Carmen.

'What the hell was Susan into, Jack?'

'Some very heavy stuff, going by the money hidden at the pool. It was a clever place to stash the notes but Susan's house suffered as they became more desperate to find it.'

'Do you think she knew it was there?'

'Maybe, maybe not. Depends on how deep she was in. She could have been used or she was part of an organisation generating huge amounts of cash, but something went badly wrong for her. It all has to link in to her death. If she knew where the cash was and wouldn't say, then she paid the ultimate price. If it wasn't to do with the money, then she may have crossed someone.'

Eva looked ahead as they slowed again for stationary traffic. 'But why go to such elaborate lengths to murder her? I mean, she may not have pulled in for the guy in the yellow jacket and the guy coming out of the top window may have missed the car.'

Jack had stopped the car behind the queue. 'If she was part of some drug-dealing organisation it could have been a way of removing two problem people. We'll have to wait for the post mortem results on the faller. It could take some time to identify him, but toxicology results could tell us something. Tests will show if he was alive when he fell.'

'You mean he was murdered too?'

'Can't be ruled out. The bed wasn't slept in and the room hadn't been used.'

'Oh, my God. How bad can this get?'

Eva fell silent again for the rest of the drive and Jack concentrated on negotiating the traffic. As he thought through the events of the day, he didn't want to tell her how bad this could get.

Chapter Eleven

Salvador took the Madrid exit from the motorway and headed for the Vallecas district. After ten minutes he turned right into a small street surrounded by run-down properties and graffiti. He slowed as he approached another small road on his right and drove in towards a row of lock-ups. He stopped just before a faded blue garage door and the hot night air hit him as he lowered his window. Switching off his engine he waited and listened. Only the ticking of his engine disturbed the silence and when he was sure there was no one around he opened the door and approached the lock-up.

There were two large padlocks to open at each side and he unlocked them with his left hand before hefting the door up and over with his right. Checking inside, he switched on a small overhead bulb before walking back to the car. Sliding back behind the wheel he started the engine and quietly drove the car inside. He pulled the garage door down and clicked it shut. It took him ten minutes to prise open the wing mirrors and remove the bags. He put the mirrors back as he had found them and placed the two small bags into a black rucksack. Removing the keys from the ignition, he slung the bag over his shoulder, switched off the light and quietly opened the door.

Everything was completely still as he wiped down the interior of the car and the inside panels. Stepping out he rubbed the cloth vigorously round the wing mirrors before sticking it in his pocket. He looked around and nodded to himself before walking out of the garage and locking the overhead door with both padlocks. He wiped the locks and the outside of the door before throwing the cloth into a small waste bin and strolled away without a backward glance. After he turned the corner he walked towards a Seat Leon parked on waste ground across the road and pulled a cigarette pack from his pocket and lit up. His first Marlborough in over an hour. Inhaling deeply he reached the car and felt under the front right wheel arch. The keys were taped to the inside panel and in a minute he was in the driver's seat. Once inside, he opened the glove compartment and retrieved his new untraceable phone.

As he pulled away, a wave of relief washed over him. He was free of Vicente's tracking and had a full tank of fuel in a car unconnected to the mob. Only Frank knew of the switch and as far as Rico he was knew he was still in the Audi. No one was looking for a red Leon. He missed the trappings of the car he'd just abandoned, but he smiled to himself. He was now anonymous and would be rich beyond his wildest dreams.

***

Vicente did the only thing he knew when stressed, and at midnight the club was in full swing when he arrived. After three brandies he left the bar and headed out into the action on the floor. Three girls were dancing to house music and he joined them. After ten minutes he signalled them to leave the floor and they all followed him back to the bar. As he pulled out his wad of notes they shouted out their drinks orders.

Vicente pointed out a table in the corner and after they'd all chosen their seats their drinks arrived. He flashed his money again as he over-tipped the waitress and the girls looked at each other and smiled. He kept the drinks flowing and as the crowd began to thin around 2am he announced, 'All back to my place.'

The taxi dropped them at his apartment and Vicente helped the giggling girls out and paid off the driver. As the girls flopped on the sofas, he brought out two bottles of Prosecco and began pouring it into glasses. The music pulsated through the large open-plan room and two of the girls started dancing. The third moved across to where Vicente was leaning against his bar, watching. 'How about a dance?'

'Sure.' Her pupils were dilated and he wondered what she'd had in the last few hours. The girl pulled him closer and he felt her hips grind into him.

'What's your name?'

'Maria. You're Vicente, yes?'

'That's right.'

'I haven't seen you at the club for a while.'

'Too busy making money.'

Dancing with her, he felt his tensions begin to fade. After a while, he went over to the bar and he noticed the two other girls sitting closely on the sofa and laughing.

He poured out two brandies and said to Maria, 'The girls seem to like each other, why don't we leave them to it?' He guided her through to his bedroom holding a brandy glass in each hand.

He awoke at six o'clock and stretched out his arm but there was nobody there. As he walked naked into the living room he saw a mess of empty bottles and half-full glasses littering the room and groaned.

The cold shower helped bring his thoughts into focus and he lurched out to dry himself before struggling into a black satin dressing gown. As he tried to gather his thoughts after the night of noisy sex and booze, he realised Salvador should at least have reached Madrid. He would be his first call after he found the coffee in the messed-up kitchen.

***

Jack's only slender lead apart from Vicente were the wholesalers who had originally supplied Beach Babe. Maybe they'd met Susan. They may even have heard of Vicente. He went online and looked for beauty product wholesalers within a five-mile radius of Malaga. On his sixth call to a company named Jade Beauty he asked to speak to the owner.

'My name is Jack Barclay and I'm a private detective. I was wondering if you could help me?'

'I'll try. I'm Vicky.'

Jack knew she was British, having a hint of a London accent.

'I wondered if you'd had any business dealings with a company called Beach Babe?'

'Oh yes, I know them quite well. Susan is really switched on and good fun.'

'So, you knew Susan?'

'Yes, we've had a few long lunches and we went out on the town one night a few weeks ago.' She paused. 'Did you just say knew Susan?'

'Yes, I'm afraid Susan is dead. I'm very sorry. That's why I'm calling. I'm just trying to get some background information on her.'

'Oh, my God, that's shocking news. I can hardly believe it. What happened?'

'Can I come over and see you? I'm in Malaga at the moment?'

'Yes, please do. We're on the industrial estate on the road to Alhaurín de la Torre.'

'I can be there in about an hour.'

'I'll be here.'

An hour later Jack pulled into the small industrial estate and stopped at the direction board just inside the entrance. Jade was in unit twelve and he followed the numbers until he came to it. A black BMW M3 convertible with the top down was parked outside and he pulled in next to it.

He rang the bell outside the office and waited. A voice came from the box fixed next to the door. 'Who is it?'

'Jack Barclay. I called you an hour ago.'

There was a soft click and the door opened. The small reception area was decorated in pastel shades and photographs of young models adorned the walls. A door opened at the back of the room and a woman who looked to be in her late thirties walked towards him. She had striking jet-black cropped hair and wore a mint-coloured T-shirt and a short black skirt.

'I'm Vicky.' Jack stretched out his right hand and she shook it while frowning at him. 'I'm still reeling at the news you gave me. Please come through to the office.'

It was small and the decor was similar in appearance to the reception area. Through a window in the far wall he could see a warehouse of sorts with lots of boxes stacked up and shelves filled with colourful bottles and spray cans.

Vicky pulled up a chair and said, 'Please.'

Jack opened by saying how sorry he was to bring such news. 'It has come as a terrible shock to her family and friends.'

'What happened, Mr Barclay?'

'Susan died in London just over two weeks ago. She was in her car when someone fell out of a high window onto her roof. She was crushed and we think she died instantly.'

'That is really awful.' Vicky went silent and then said, 'It's also very bizarre, don't you think?'

'I do and so do some others. We're waiting for the results of post mortems and other forensic tests. I'm here in Malaga with her sister, Eva, who doesn't think it was an accident.'

'Do you think the same?'

He nodded. 'There are some unusual aspects surrounding the way in which she found herself under the path of a man falling from a high hotel window. There are a lot of things we don't know and I'm hoping you'll be able to give me some background on Susan's life in Malaga.'

'I'll do my best. We weren't close friends but we enjoyed each other's company and as I said, we hit the town one night a few weeks ago. Finished up in a nightclub.'

'Did you know any of her friends?'

'She didn't talk much about her private life to me but I had the impression she had made friends through the beauty business. She was always being invited to parties here and in Marbella. I remember her telling me she had partied on a yacht in Puerto Banús until dawn a couple of months ago. I don't know where she found all the energy.'

'So, she had boyfriends?'

'Yes, she enjoyed male company but never spoke of anyone being special.'

'Did you know she made trips to London a few times a year?'

'Yes, she said they were business trips. She didn't like flying so usually drove. It's a long way but she said she loved the freedom she felt when on the open road.'

'Going back to her friends, did she ever mention someone called Vicente?'

Jack watched as she thought about the question. 'I can't be too sure but the name rings a bell. The night we went to the nightclub she ignored a call on her mobile as we were heading in through the door. The doorman had recognised her and waved us in. As we made for the bar her phone rang again and she stopped and placed her other hand over her ear to try and hear the caller. It was a hell of a din as I'm sure you can imagine. I waited next to her and heard her say where she was. She killed the call quickly but I'm sure she said something like, 'Bloody Vince.' We made it to the bar and started on the champagne but the call had put her on edge for a few minutes. After another couple of drinks she returned to her normal self.'

'Did you ever hear her mention the name again?'

'No, never.'

'Can you give me the name of the nightclub.'

'Sure. It was Bianca's. Quite a few ex-pats use it and it's a bit of a pick-up club but it's well run and the music's good.'

Jack made a mental note of the name and moved on. 'This might seem a bit of an unusual question, but how well do you think Susan's business was doing?'

'It's a very competitive scene here in the beauty world. There is so much money around but margins are cut right back to stay alive. Even the rich people are shopping online because they can buy cheaper and it saves them the hassle of driving to the shopping malls. Susan seemed well connected but her business must have been suffering like everyone else's as online business took off in a big way. I think I know why you're asking.'

'Why?'

'She was living very well. Fabulous clothes, a luxury car and of course her villa. I often wondered how she managed to fund her lifestyle. I work hard and have a good income but she was way out of my league. She was generous and money never seemed to be a worry.'

As Jack listened, he looked Vicky straight in the eye. 'Where do you think she was making her money?'

She said nothing for a few seconds. 'I really don't know, but she was so cagey about lots of things and I think she may have been involved in something dodgy. When we were together either during business hours or socially, her mobile phone was always going off. She never once took any of the calls and if it was a message, she'd read it and carry on as if nothing had happened. I assumed she replied to the callers when I wasn't around. It was a bit unusual.'

Jack had one more question for her. 'Do you think Susan took drugs?'

Vicky paused before answering. 'A lot of people dabble in a social way especially at parties and there are plenty of them. I can't say for sure but she did sometimes disappear to the toilets and come back looking very happy. I don't use myself but it's no big deal around the social scene here and they're easy to come by. Everyone knows someone who can supply. Just like going to the corner shop.' Jack nodded, familiar with this scenario.

Vicky quickly added, 'Everyone except me that is,' and laughed. 'If Susan wasn't using, then she'd be in the minority, but that's just my opinion, so please don't quote me.'

Jack was sure he wouldn't get much more from her and said, 'Thank you for being so candid. We're at the beginning of our investigation at the moment. Here's my card, Vicky. If you hear of anything or think of anything you may have missed please just give me a call.' He stood up and shook her hand.

'I'll do that and I hope you find out why Susan died. She was a lovely lady.'

Jack walked out to his car and Googled 'Bianca's' on his phone. He wrote down the address and phone number and reversed out of the small parking space. Vicente was still his only lead.

Chapter Twelve

Salvador headed out of Madrid and joined the A2 for Zaragoza and Barcelona. The rucksack was on the floor in front of the passenger seat and he glanced down at it as he lit a cigarette from the lighter under the radio.

He could feel the tiredness creeping up on him and he decided to stop at the next motel. He pulled in twenty minutes later and parked up near the back of the already crowded car park in front of a small two-storey motel. He grabbed his rucksack and walked back to reception. They had three rooms left and he took the one nearest his car and paid in cash. The reception area looked well used but clean and after the bored-looking young man behind the desk passed him his key he made his way towards his room. Vending machines in the corridor offered crisps and chocolates and he thumbed in ten euros for some instant food. He used the last of his change for a cappuccino in a cardboard cup and winced as he lifted the hot container from the machine.

After his shower he placed the rucksack beside him under the sheet, linked his arm through one of the straps and fell into a deep sleep. Seven hours later the sun shone in through his open curtains and he got up and dressed. He was back on the road in ten minutes and aimed to be in Barcelona by nightfall.

It was Jack and Eva's second night in Hotel Carmen and Jack knew she was hoping for more information. More hope that Susan's death could be explained. It was 5pm and Jack had just returned from seeing Vicky.

'Let's go out tonight, Eva. I've been recommended to a place not far from here and we can book a table.'

'Sounds good. I'm hungry so let's make it early. Maybe something like seven.'

Jack knew that was very early for the Spanish but it would give him the opportunity to have a quiet conversation with his client. He hadn't much to tell her in the way of progress.

Their taxi dropped them at El Pescador at 7pm and Jack escorted Eva through the front door. It was a traditional Andalusian restaurant and they were shown to a table well inside next to a small stage. They grimaced at one another and asked for a table set away from the centre of the room. It was a generous menu but they decided to share a paella and a bottle of Edalo white wine made from local grapes. After the waiter had opened the wine and filled their glasses, they clinked them.

'I don't know how long I'll be able to stay in Malaga, Jack. I don't even know when I'll be able to get back into Susan's villa.'

Jack nodded. 'I think the forensic people will be examining things inside as they search for evidence. That would involve the removal of floor boards and wall panels. You name it, they'll probably remove it. It's impossible to know when we'll get back in. They may stake it out and see if anyone comes back on the trail of the money. I'm pretty sure they'll put some hidden cameras inside the villa and by the pool. You may have to return to London and come back when you are able to gain access for your sister's personal stuff. The amount of cash found by the pool will have escalated the whole investigation. It's going to very difficult for you.'

Eva raised her wine glass and said, 'I lead such a mundane life and suddenly this happens. It's unbelievable really.'

'What do you do exactly?' Jack asked.

'I work for a company in Islington. They market pharmaceutical products and specialise in the field of mental health. It's booming, unfortunately.'

'So, what's your role in the company?'

'Oh, I'm PA to the Marketing Director. It's long hours but he's great to work for. He's got a sense of humour.'

'Do you live alone?'

'You can tell?'

'I didn't mean it that way. It's just that you never mention anyone else in your life.'

'I've been married but it didn't work out. I was young and it was a mistake and a bit painful but our break up was amicable. I'm quite happy on my own. Well, most of the time.'

They stopped talking as the paella arrived with some drama and a table was set up next to them. The waiter served Eva then Jack and topped up their wine glasses before leaving. Nothing was said as they started eating their meal.

Jack put down his knife and fork and dabbed his mouth with his napkin. 'Were you sorry when your sister went to live in Spain?'

Eva stopped eating and looked up. 'Yes, I was. We were pretty close but I think we were always conscious of the difference in our personalities. I used to envy her ability to attract people and I suppose I lived in her shadow to some extent, but we knew we loved each other. I threw myself into my job after I became single again and I didn't know everything about her life in Spain because we'd drifted apart. She was living in a small rented apartment in those days and her business seemed to be picking up. I visited her a couple of times and slept on the sofa in her flat. Once she asked me if I'd like to join her in Spain but I said it was a step too far for me. I think she missed me more than she admitted. Back then, I wish I'd kept in touch with her more often. I think she had gone into debt to get her beauty business going but I was a little scared to ask.'

'What do you mean by that?'

'I realise now I was only allowed to know so much about her and I did begin to think she was being evasive. I often wondered how she could be so generous if her business was still having growing pains but she was such good company on our nights out

I just let it go. Sometimes she used to try and fix me up with dates but I told her I was happy to be single again.'

Jack stretched his hand out to cover Eva's on the table. 'You could never know about her life. Unbeknown to you I suspect she was involved with some very dangerous people by then. Maybe it was better you didn't know.'

They finished their meal and after a short silence Jack said, 'I'm working later tonight. We'll go back to the hotel and then I'll take off.'

'Where are you going?'

'I have a lead on Vicente. It shouldn't take long and I'll see you for breakfast.'

'Well, be careful, Jack.'

The taxi dropped them off at the Hotel Carmen and Jack asked the driver to wait while he accompanied Eva inside. When he climbed back in the taxi he asked for Bianca's.

***

Jack paid off the taxi outside the club and approached the door. There was only one bouncer on duty and by the looks of things he wasn't very busy.

'Okay to go in?'

'Sure. It's quiet so far.'

The entrance fee included a drink and Jack made for the bar. He sat on a high stool with a whisky and water and watched the scene around him. He estimated the crowd to be around one hundred, mainly young girls. No one took much notice of a thirty-nine-year-old, but that suited him. In one corner a crowd of girls were creating a lot of attention and from the sounds drifting over they were British. Their table was loaded with cocktails and with one wearing a sign saying virgin on her T-shirt, Jack assumed it was a hen party. The music was some rap stuff he didn't understand but then he wasn't here to like the place. He drained his drink and caught the bar tender's eye.

'Yes, sir.'

'Same again. Ice please.'

'No worries.'

When he returned, Jack handed him a twenty-euro note and told him to keep the change. The man gave him an odd look but Jack quickly said, 'I'm looking for an old friend who uses this place. I thought you could help me.'

'You a cop?'

'No, I used to work with this guy, but we've lost touch. I'm here on holiday.'

'Who are you looking for?'

'His name is Vicente. It's been so long I can't remember his second name.'

'Yeah, I know Vicente.' Then he stood looking at Jack and said nothing.

Jack took out his wallet and removed another twenty and laid it on the bar.

The barman said, 'I've got to be careful here. Your money says you're a cop or close to one. He's an important guy around here and I don't know you.'

'I'm a private investigator and it's only background I'm after.'

'Okay, but this conversation never took place. I only know he's a regular here and he likes the girls in a big way. He usually pulls tourists who are looking for some holiday excitement and they sure get it with Vicente. He's a big spender and as far as I know has a great place to take them back to. In terms of his bar tab he's about the biggest customer we have.'

'Do you know where he lives?'

'I think he has a place here in Malaga but he also brags about his villa by the sea in Sierra Blanca.'

'What about his surname?'

The barman hesitated then said, 'Perez and before you ask anything else he tells everyone he is in import and export. Something to do with swimming pools.'

Jack said, 'Okay, last one. Which nights does he usually come in?'

'Varies, but often he's here on a Friday and Saturday. Lots of tourists are in. Look I gotta go. Customers waiting.' He picked up the twenty and moved down the bar.

Jack finished his whisky and made for the door. A middle-aged blonde-haired woman from the hen party reached out and tried to pull him onto the dance floor. '

'Come on handsome.' He smiled and kept going.

The hot night air hit him as he exited onto the street and he turned to the bouncer and handed him a piece of paper with his mobile number written on it. A fifty-euro note was tucked inside. He said, 'There's more where that came from if you'd give me a call when Vicente next comes into the club.'

The bouncer nodded and flagged down an empty taxi as it was about to leave the kerb.

Jack climbed in. 'Hotel Carmen, please.' Malaga nightlife was an expensive business.

Chapter Thirteen

Vicente had left two messages for Salvador, but he hadn't responded. The tracker said he was between Madrid and Burgos, so he was well behind schedule. Why the fuck wasn't he replying? He left it for half an hour and rang him again. Straight to message. The sweat on his face was nothing to do with the outside temperature and he began pacing up and down in his kitchen as he tried to figure out what might be happening. He called Frank. 'Have you heard from Salvador?'

'Nope, not a thing.'

'Okay, ring him now and call me back.'

Vicente's mobile rang in a couple of minutes. 'No reply. It went straight to message. What's the problem?'

'He's not picking up. The tracker says he's north of Madrid. That's all I know.'

'Let's give it a bit longer, Vicente. Anything could have happened.'

'That's what's worrying me.'

He ended the call and Googled traffic conditions on the A1. There had been some small hold-ups due to minor accidents but all traffic was reported as moving well. He checked the tracker again and its location was further north. Vicente relaxed a little and rang Salvador's mobile again and left another message. 'Where the fuck are you? Call me now.' He went across to his drinks cabinet and pulled out a bottle of Soberano. Pouring a large measure into a goblet, he knocked it back in one. He sat down on the couch with a second and closed his eyes.

***

Salvador was making good time and was over half way to Zaragoza on the A2. He pulled in for fuel and bought a hamburger and chips to take out. Driving round to the rear of the building he stopped under the shade of a large oak tree at the back of the parking area. He finished eating and picked up his new phone, which had been charging. The number he punched answered on the second ring.

'Frank, it's Salvador. I'm one hour from Zaragoza. I'll make Barcelona by early evening. Have you heard from Vicente?'

Frank let out a small chuckle. 'Yeah, he rang about half an hour ago. He's shitting himself. Did all go well with the switch?'

'Yeah, all to plan. The tracker and my phone are on a truck that was parked up. Don't know where he's headed and the stuff is with me.'

'Good. How's the car?'

'It's fine. Not an Audi A6, but it's running well and no one is looking for a Seat Leon. I'm anonymous now. Feels good.'

'You should rest up in Barcelona? You have a long drive tomorrow.'

'I'll find a small hotel somewhere.'

'Okay, but don't forget the rucksack in the morning.'

'No chance. I put one of my shoes inside it and it sleeps with me.'

Frank laughed. 'I like that. Keep to all the speed limits and call me tomorrow after you put some miles in. This is a big one so any problems ring me.'

'Will do.'

Salvador checked his watch and calculated he'd be in Barcelona by 5pm. He was looking forward to a shower and a good meal. He'd make it an early night and leave before dawn to get as close to Paris as possible tomorrow.

Chapter Fourteen

Jack started his search for Vicente by using one of his private databases. It had been expensive to buy and almost as much to keep it updated but it usually gave him something. He entered his complex security codes and began with a narrowed-down search for Vicente Perez, Malaga. The response was positive and Jack saw his first image of the man he was looking for. The photo had been taken at a distance but it showed a dark-haired man walking with a woman by a marina. He was smartly dressed in light-coloured expensive-looking casual clothes and the woman was looking up at him and smiling as if he'd just said something funny.

He moved to a different section within the database to look for more detail. There was one ancient conviction of assault but no record of any sentence passed. Jack searched for his whereabouts and found an address in the Sierra Blanca area of Marbella. There was no mention of an address in Malaga. He noted the address down and moved on to Vicente's background. He'd been born into to a working-class family in Algeciras and moved to live with an aunt in Malaga when he was fifteen. He drifted around and was thought to have been involved in petty theft before graduating to the criminal class in Malaga until the age of eighteen. There was no information on him after that.

Jack took out his credit card and after entering his details, requested an update on Vicente. It took about thirty seconds and the flashed message said, 'Vicente Perez may now be involved in drug-related organised crime on the Costa Del Sol. There is no further information at this time.' Jack typed in 'Known associates?' and waited. The return message said, 'No known associates.'

The thoughts churned around in his head because this information confirmed he was dealing with class A drugs. Vicente had to be using Susan to ferry stuff to the UK. She was good-looking and personable and she needed his financial help to maintain her lifestyle in Spain. What better mule to have on the payroll. So why did she die in London? If Susan had mixed pleasure with business and talked too much, she'd paid the ultimate price. That's how it looked to him and the next move was a meeting with Vicente. He looked at his note and put Vicente's address into a route planner on his mobile. Then he Googled Sierra Blanca real estate and found first-line properties starting at two million euros. Not bad for a guy from humble beginnings in Algeciras.

Jack woke at 7am and showered. He'd track Vicente today and Eva needed to understand he had to be on his own. He called her room.

'Eva, it's Jack. Good morning.'

'Hi, what's with the early call?'

'I have things to do today that you shouldn't be involved with and I just wanted to tell you.'

'Like what, Jack?'

'Can we talk about it over breakfast?'

'Sounds good. About twenty minutes?'

'I'll see you down there.'

Jack showered and then checked his phone messages. There was nothing of importance and he went down to the restaurant. Eva arrived five minutes later and Jack couldn't help but smile as he took in her appearance. She was wearing tight white trousers and a light-blue top and she had pulled her hair into a loose ponytail.

'Morning.'

'Good morning, Eva. Sleep well?'

'It could have been a lot better.' She looked him in the eyes and sat down.

Jack signalled to the waiter and asked for coffee.

'So, what's on the agenda today?' Eva asked.

Jack sipped his coffee and said, 'Well, your agenda could be a swim in the pool.'

'And yours?'

'I'm going after Vicente.'

'You know where he is?'

'I can't be sure, but I know where he lives so I'll start there. I won't be confronting him yet but I'd like to know where he goes during the day and I hope to get some shots of him.'

'So, when will I see you?'

'I'll call you on my way back.'

They chose from the cold buffet and Jack looked at his watch as Eva finished her breakfast.

'I need to be going, Eva. I'll see you tonight. Hope you'll be okay.'

'I'll be fine, Jack. Just take care of yourself.'

They left the restaurant and Eva went back to her room. Jack walked to the hotel's small car park and unlocked the hire car. Setting his sat nav he drove out into the traffic and followed the directions for Vicente's home in Marbella. He estimated it was about an hour away.

Jack cruised past the gate and noted the position of Vicente's villa. It was the second in a row of six. Front line to the Mediterranean with nothing to spoil the view. The property was hidden by a solid wooden double gate and he drove on, pulling into the side of the road after a quarter of a mile. Choosing a spot not overlooked by villas, he turned and parked a hundred yards from Vicente's home and checked his camera, setting it for a zoom-in on the outside of the gate. He was used to long surveillance but usually in colder climes. He kept the engine running and notched up the AC. The radio was on a local station and low. His Cannon lay on his lap and he kept his gaze firmly on Vicente's front entrance. At midday he saw the gates begin to slide slowly open and he raised his camera. A black Audi Q7 exited left and Jack squeezed off six shots of the driver's head profile and one of the rear registration plate. Waiting until the vehicle neared the end of the road Jack moved forward slowly and started following.

The Audi seemed to be heading for the centre of Malaga and as the traffic became heavier Jack was finding it difficult to keep the vehicle in sight. He had to stop for a red light and the Audi made it through. The last he saw was the target in the distance turning right at a large sign for Guadalhorce Industrial Estate. Jack carried on anyway and took a right at the sign. It took an hour of driving around but he eventually spotted the Audi parked half out of sight at the side of a small scruffy-looking garage.

The doors were closed and the sign above said La Pintura. Jack smiled as he knew the words meant 'work of art'. There were two other cars parked outside, one having been masked up at the back ready for a paint spray. He drove past, then turned back before finding a place to park on the opposite side of the road near the garage. Sliding down in the driver's seat he took some shots of the garage and the Audi parked at the side.

The man he took to be Vicente came out in about half an hour, scowling as he walked away. Jack managed to get a better shot of his face before he drove off and he decided to wait and see if anyone else came out. A few minutes later a middle-aged man wearing paint-spattered white overalls walked outside and opened the garage door before climbing into the car with the masking tape and filler in its rear wing. Jack raised his camera and took frontal shots of him as the man drove slowly forward before getting out and closing the door. After waiting for five minutes, Jack started his engine and began the drive through late-afternoon traffic to the Hotel Carmen. He thought he'd made a little progress.

Chapter Fifteen

Salvador saw a sign for Orleans and knew he was getting close to Paris. He'd make Calais the next day. It had been a long drive and he was feeling tired. He took the Orleans exit and began looking for a secluded spot off the main road. His headlights found an unfenced track to his left and he slowed before turning into it. He could see it led to a field and the only light came from a pale moon. The LED torch was in the driver's door pocket and picking up his rucksack he opened the door and stepped out. In the light of the torch he found the screwdriver in the outside pocket of the rucksack and began easing off the wing mirror on the driver's side. Inside the prepared space he pushed in one of the bags and carefully replaced the casing. Moving round to the other side he repeated the operation and finished by wiping down both mirrors with a clean cloth. Shining his torch, he saw a large thicket of high bushes and began inching his way in. He could feel the thorns cutting him but he kept going for another few yards. He threw the rucksack as far as he could into a dense part of the bushes before retreating to his car. Inside he dabbed the blood from his hands and wrists and pulled out the thorns sticking into his flesh. Reversing, he found an opening to another field. He turned the car round and killed his lights. He'd park up and sleep inside his car tonight and set off before dawn. Tomorrow he'd be in London. Scrolling down to Frank he texted that he'd let him know his ferry time when he reached Calais. Reclining his seat, he threw a rug over himself, closed his eyes and hoped for a few hours' sleep.

***

Jack reached the hotel at 5pm. He rang Eva's room but didn't get a reply and hung up. She rang him back almost immediately. 'Sorry, Jack I must have dropped off. How was your day?'

'It all went pretty well. Found a few things out. What time should we eat?'

'I've reserved a table for 7pm and I've booked a taxi. Surprise destination.'

'Sounds good. I've some work to do here so I'll see you in reception.'

'Let's meet at 6.45. See you later.'

Jack switched on his laptop and Googled La Pintura garage in Guadalhorce, Malaga. He recognised the photograph of the frontage from his visit and the entry said they specialise in bodywork repairs. The owner was Juan Garcia. Jack noted down the address and phone number. Then he clicked on Google earth and searched for Vicente's villa. The setting was as magnificent as it had looked today and Jack was specifically interested in the beach fronting the properties. From zooming in it looked as if the property was accessible from the beach and he saw no private signs. Vicente's villa was gated at the rear with a high hedge screening the pool area from anyone walking along the shore. Jack grunted with satisfaction. There were no obvious signs of security around the hedge but that didn't mean there wasn't any. He used his camera to take a photograph of the Google image on his screen. He checked his watch and quickly removed the USB card reader from his camera and connected it by OTG cable to his iPhone. In a few seconds he'd transferred the head shot photos of Vicente and Juan to his mobile. He put it on charge and walked through to the bathroom for a shower.

He was waiting in the lobby when Eva walked out of the lift and he almost did a double take. Her black off-the-shoulder dress was so tight he wondered how she'd managed to get into it.

'You look terrific tonight.'

'Thank you. You've scrubbed up pretty well yourself.' She smiled at him as they walked outside. 'Our taxi's here.'

The taxi climbed up the narrow streets of the old town and the restaurant Eva had chosen was the El Mirador. She had asked for a good table and heads turned as she walked through the restaurant. Their table was tucked away in a small balcony with a breath-taking view over the old town. The evening was hot and the sounds of the city drifted up. They both ordered steak with a bottle of Rioja Contador, which the *camarero de vino* assured them was one of the best in the house.

Jack picked up a black olive and watched as Eva did the same. 'So, how was the pool?'

'Lovely, thank you. It was good to relax. I was going to do some clothes shopping but idleness took over. I skipped lunch and decided to wait until now to eat. I hope it's a big steak.'

'Did you have a good day?'

Jack paused and said, 'It was a reconnaissance day really, but very fruitful. I scoped out Vicente's villa and then followed him to a small garage on an industrial estate that could also prove interesting. I'll be visiting both these places again in the next few days but not by invitation.'

The waiter arrived with their wine and they whispered 'Cheers' as they clinked glasses after he left.

Just as he was about to bring his phone out and show her the day's photos, their steaks arrived. They were huge. A platter of vegetables and frites followed and their table suddenly became very crowded.

'No portion control here, Jack. This is lovely.'

As they enjoyed their meal Eva said, 'So you think we're getting somewhere?'

'Oh, yes. I'm sure Vicente and his garage man are mixed up in all of this. I just have to find out why. I have some suspicions, but I will need to dig deeper over the next few days. I'm afraid you won't see too much of me and I wouldn't blame you if you wanted to go back to London.'

'I've spoken to my boss and explained things and I'll do a bit of work from here on my laptop. I'm okay for a few days more and I do want to visit Susan's home just to straighten the pictures if nothing else. Anyway, I was hoping we could mix in a little pleasure to ease the pain of it all.' She looked straight at Jack as she said it.

Jack smiled. 'I haven't had much pleasure lately.'

'Maybe you're working too hard.'

Jack sipped some water. 'When my marriage failed I threw myself even deeper into my investigation business. It was time spent working away that had caused many of the problems in the first place. I mean, my phone could go right now and I'd have to leave. It goes with the territory.'

'I'd understand.'

'But would you, though? It's okay the first few times then it becomes a real issue. Maybe that's the reason I haven't had a serious relationship since my divorce. It was all very painful.'

'Well, I enjoy your company, Jack, so let's mix in a bit of pleasure.'

They finished their steaks and told the waiter they'd have a break before dessert. Eva said she'd read in a travel magazine that the crème brûlées at this restaurant were to die for.

Jack relaxed as he watched her order the desserts. He could see she was enjoying the evening and the heady mix of the red wine and the ambience of the restaurant was beginning to lower her inhibitions.

Laughter from nearby bars filled the humid night air and they began strolling around the old town after they left the restaurant. Eva linked her arm through Jack's as they negotiated a rough part of the cobbled street and to anyone passing, they looked like a loved-up couple. A small bar caught their attention and they headed towards it for a nightcap. They were about to go in when Jack's phone rang.

'It's Diego from the door at Bianca's. He's in.' The line went dead.

Jack turned round to Eva and said, 'I have to work tonight.'

'Okay.' They carried on to a small square with a taxi rank and Eva asked for the Hotel Carmen. 'Are you coming back to the hotel?'

'Yes, I need to pick up a couple of things.' The ride was about ten minutes and when they entered the lobby Jack said, 'I'll see you for breakfast.'

'Whatever you are doing tonight please take care.'

'I will and I'm sorry to spoil things.'

'It's okay. Honestly.'

Jack made his way to his room and collected a small rucksack, packing a torch, a penknife, a pair of cotton gloves, a baseball cap and a length of wire. He took the lift back to the basement and placed the rucksack under his seat in the car. He drove out and headed for Sierra Blanca.

He parked short of the road leading down to the beach then he put on his dark blue baseball cap and stuffed the gloves into his pocket. The rucksack was so light he could hardly feel it on his shoulders and he pulled the cap well down over his face and began walking. A partial moon threw pale light onto the deserted beach and he hugged the hedges as he made his way to the back of Vicente's villa. When he reached it he stopped and listened, but the only sound was the lapping of the Mediterranean waves a hundred yards away. He walked along the hedge and just as he reached the end, found a small gap.

Bending down, he pulled at the foliage just above the roots and widened the gap. The hole he created would just about be wide enough for him to go through and he laid his rucksack and cap on the sand. Crouching, he could smell stale urine and wondered which type of animal had started the tunnelling in the first place. He managed to wriggle his shoulders through and felt the stinging on his arms as he was jabbed by the branches. It took about two minutes before he was finally in Vicente's garden and he retrieved his rucksack and cap before crouching and studying the layout of the garden. The villa and swimming pool were in complete darkness and Jack stuck his cap back on, pulling it right down over his face.

Keeping to the side hedge he began to make his way up the garden, looking for security cameras as he neared the pool. He could see no obvious sign of security and wondered if Vicente hadn't got round to installing it. Skirting round the covered pool he saw a security light fixed high up on the back of the property and he stayed by the hedge and hoped he was out of its range. He made the side of the villa and crept round towards what seemed like an extension to the main building. Looking in through a window he saw a treadmill and weights sitting on their stands.

Jack put on his gloves before switching on his torch and running his finger round the window frame. In the penetrating LED light he could see no sign of it being wired and he searched in the rucksack for his penknife. The lock was a simple one and he edged the blade in and made contact with the handle and began levering it up. He heard a click and pushed the window open a fraction. There was no screeching alarm and he pushed the window with more force. It opened fully and Jack knew he was in. Tossing the rucksack in, he climbed up and pushing the blind to one side, crawled through, jumping down onto a polished wooden floor. He shone his torch around the walls and still couldn't see any security so he carried on towards the door. He was in a narrow corridor and carried on until he came to the stairs. Still no alarms going off. The upstairs was sectioned off into four bedrooms and he found the master. It was decorated in a contemporary style with whites and reds dominating and Jack went to the chest of drawers on the far wall and began searching. There was nothing of interest and nothing taped underneath the drawers. There were three paintings on the walls and Jack slid them all to one side but there was nothing behind any of them. He lifted the rug but there was only the tiled floor. He repeated the exercise in the other bedrooms but came up with nothing. Inching his way downstairs, he used the torch to check for any movement sensors or cameras but saw none.

The living room was also done in a contemporary theme and he checked all the drawers and cupboards but found nothing of interest. The kitchen was immaculate and with a half-empty fridge he deduced that Vicente wasn't big on cooking. A side door led to the internal garage and he walked in. There were no vehicles but Jack detected the smell of carbon monoxide so maybe he'd driven to Malaga tonight. His mind went back to the find of jewellery in the bag of bark in the UK recently and he shone his torch around the interior. The beam picked up a trunk in the far corner and he walked over to it. There was a large padlock on the clasp and Jack used his penknife to open it in about twenty seconds. Inside he saw bags and small plastic containers variously filled with screws, bolts, drill heads and all the bits and pieces the DIY enthusiast would need. Sticking his hand in he found the depth to be only around twelve inches before he felt a floor. He unloaded some of the containers and saw a wooden platform. He prised it up and saw the hidden contents. Money. Jack knew he was looking at many thousands of euros. He stuck his hand in between the tied wads and came to another shelf. Lifting that, he saw wood shavings and he rummaged in them until his hand felt what he thought was plastic. The bag he brought out must have weighed a quarter of a kilo. Jack knew it was probably cocaine. He took three images of the find on his camera phone and put everything back as he'd found it. Using the torch, he double-checked there was no debris around the trunk and snapped the padlock back into place. Backtracking through the house, he left by the way he came in and used his knife to ease the window handle down after he'd climbed out. He'd left a few scratches on the window frame and he rubbed out the worst with the back of his gloved hand. He scuffed up the earth he'd been standing on and within minutes he was back on the beach.

The moon had been obscured by cloud as he tried to re-arrange the hedge branches as best he could then he made his way back to the car. The whole operation had taken twenty minutes. His drive back to Malaga was uneventful and he walked into the lobby of the Carmen at 1am.

***

Eva rang Jack at 7.30am. 'I've been worried.'

'No need. All went well. I was late back and didn't want to disturb you.'

'I was awake and just hoped to hear from you.'

'I'm sorry. How about some breakfast?'

'I'll need about fifteen minutes.'

'See you in the lobby.'

He told her everything that had happened and she was genuinely shocked when he came to the part about the trunk. 'So this is about drugs as you thought. How on earth did Susan get involved in all this?'

Jack shrugged and said, 'The money can be irresistible.'

'But what of the people whose lives are going to be ruined?'

'They don't think about that. But perhaps you sister wasn't aware of what was really happening. We don't know enough about the operation yet.'

'What about the stuff you found?'

'I've just rung the inspector in charge of the case. What they decide to do is up to them. They may wait for Vicente to show up at his home.'

'Did he ask you how you knew about it?'

'I just said I have reason to believe he'd find something of interest in a trunk in the garage.'

Eva raised her coffee cup and smiled.

Chapter Sixteen

It was after midnight when he pulled up at the gates, but Vicente didn't press the remote to open them. The villa was in darkness but he decided to check the property before driving in. Switching on a large torch he walked round the side of the villa and made his way down a track to the beach. As he stood on a breeze block that had been left lying on the rough grass, he peered over the hedge and shone the torchlight back and forth towards the back of the house. He felt that there was something not right and the beam finally came to rest on the blinds inside the picture window. He realised two of the slats were out of line with the others, and he knew his cleaner was meticulous about this. Stepping down, he switched off the torch and re-traced his steps before getting back into his vehicle. Throwing his Audi into reverse he edged out onto the street and accelerated away. Speeding through the empty roads he kept checking his mirror but decided he wasn't being followed. He phoned Juan and told him to meet him at the garage. 'It's after midnight, Vicente.'

'Just be there.'

By the time he reached the garage, Juan had opened up and was waiting by the main door. The A7 took up a great deal of room and Vicente saw him grimace as he squeezed in behind the huge vehicle to grab the chain and lower the garage door.

'What the fuck is up?'

Vicente didn't answer immediately but stared at Juan. 'Someone's been to my house. They may be inside right now.'

'How do you know?'

'One of the blinds has been raised. This has to be tied in to Salvador.' He picked up his phone to call him again.

Juan shook his head. 'It's the middle of the night.'

'Who gives a fuck.' Vicente rang Salvador's mobile but there was no message, no nothing. The phone was dead. He rang the tracker and got a GPS reading for Salamanca. He turned to Juan. 'Why would he change crossings? Doesn't make any sense. Shit. I bet that tracker isn't on the Audi. He's ditched it with his phone. The bastard could be anywhere. He's taken us.'

'You can't be sure of that, Vicente.'

'So how come he hasn't been in touch since he left?'

'How do I know? He could have been in a crash. He could be in a hospital somewhere. He could be dead.'

'He'd better not be.' Vicente sat down in Juan's worn old chair and threw his mobile phone onto the paint-stained table before holding his head in his hands. He knew he was as good as dead if the consignment was gone. He could almost hear Rico saying, 'Fool me once,' before putting the bullet in behind his ear.

He looked up and said, 'I need to disappear for a couple of days until I find out what's happened. Rico will call you. Just say you haven't seen me.'

'What about your vehicle?'

'Stick it round in the back yard and cover it. Have you anything here I can use?'

'There's an Alfa sitting around. It's not much but it runs okay.'

'That'll do.'

Juan opened a drawer in his desk and rummaged around. The Alfa keys were on a key ring with a silver St. Christopher tag attached. He handed them to Vicente who muttered, 'I'll need all the luck going.'

Juan indicated the car was in the yard and they left through the back door to bring it round. It was an older model Alfa Romeo in red. As Vicente climbed in he said, 'Don't contact me unless you hear from Salvador. I'll be in touch.' He quickly familiarised himself with the Alfa and drove out onto the road. As he headed for Marbella through the dark streets a feeling of doom came over him. He'd lost control and he knew he'd be hunted down.

***

Salvador joined the queue at Calais after buying a return ticket from the office at the port. His ferry would leave at 7.15pm and he'd be in London inside two hours of disembarking. He followed directions and parked his car in the bowels of the ship behind a caravan and climbed upstairs. The trip would take around ninety minutes and he managed to find a comfortable seat in the upper lounge and dozed off. The final part of his run was about to begin and it was the most dangerous. Just ahead of him was the UK Border in Dover. The vessel shuddered as the engines started up and in minutes Calais was disappearing into the distance. The dull throb of the engines began to ease his mind and he felt himself slipping into a deeper sleep.

The loudspeaker message for drivers to return to their vehicles woke him and his head jerked around as he tried to remember where he was. He made his way back down to his car and instinctively looked at the wing mirrors. All seemed to be well and he climbed in to wait for his turn to disembark. He could feel the sweat gathering in his armpits and the tension rose inside him as he drove off the ramp and followed the line of vehicles onto UK soil.

He found himself behind a 4 x 4 towing the large caravan and he felt some relief when he saw it being waved into an isolated bay by UK Border Force Officers. No one took any interest in him and he kept driving towards the exit. In his mirror he saw a sniffer dog being led to the caravan. He left the port area and approached the A20 heading towards the M20 and London. He smiled to himself as he accelerated away from Dover. He was through.

As he approached the outskirts of London he pulled into a roadside restaurant. Switching off his engine he called Frank on his mobile.

'I'm just outside London. It was a breeze at Dover.'

'You know where to come don't you?'

'Yeah. I'll probably be about an hour because of the traffic.'

'Tell me about it. See you when you get here.'

Salvador cut the call and climbed out and locked the Leon. Before walking across to the café he tapped the driver's wing mirror. It seemed solid. He ordered coffee and a bacon sandwich and was back in the car within ten minutes. The fuel gauge said three quarters and he drove out of the car park and continued north towards central London.

***

Jack's find at Vicente's villa had confirmed all his suspicions and he'd little doubt that Susan had been running class A drugs to the UK. Whether she had been under duress or threatened in some way he'd try to find out, but first he had to find Vicente. He was becoming concerned for Eva's safety now he knew the level of criminality involved. If she was unable to gain access to Susan's villa in the next twenty-four hours he was going to recommend she go back home and return to Malaga when the police had completed their forensic investigations. It was 9am and Eva had asked for her breakfast to be served in her room. When she appeared out of the lift Jack rose from his chair and waved her over. She looked stunning in a pale-yellow blouse and a cream-coloured skirt.

'Morning, Jack.'

'Good morning to you. Sleep well?'

'Pretty good. I'm not a great lover of hotel beds. Well, most of the time I'm not.'

Jack laughed and Eva joined in.

'So, where do we go today?'

'How about we have a coffee and I'll update you.'

'Okay by me.'

Jack leaned forward and said, 'I'm going to ring the police inspector in charge of the investigation and ask him when you will have access to your sister's home. If he can't be specific I'm going to suggest you return to London until such time as the villa is released to you.'

Eva looked at Jack and said, 'But I don't want to do that.'

'I know, but the criminals we are dealing with are too unpredictable and that's when things are going well. The police will be hoping they'll return to Susan's villa to search again for the money. If they thought you were in the way they'd swat you like a fly and if they thought Susan had confided in you they'd hunt you down. I wouldn't like to think how they'd get you to talk.'

Eva shuddered. 'But I don't know anything.'

'They don't know that. With the information I have, I'm going to start getting closer to these guys and it's better all round if you are not here.' He touched Eva's hand and said, 'I wouldn't ask you to leave unless I thought the danger was about to escalate.' He paused and waited for the counter argument.

'Oh, God. Okay, I'll check out today and catch a flight late afternoon or in the evening. I'm going to sleep even less now worrying about you. I can hardly believe all this.'

'Look, don't worry about me. I'll be fine, but there is something you can do for me.'

'Ask me.'

Jack pushed his empty coffee cup to the side and said, 'When Susan made one of her visits to you, were any photographs taken?'

'Yes, sometimes.'

'I'm looking for any that may have her car in the background with the registration plate in shot.'

'I've changed phones recently but I can look back when I get home. If I have anything useful I'll send them to your phone.'

'Good. Now let's find you a flight.'

***

Malaga Airport was busy and Jack parked in the short-term car park before walking Eva through to the terminal. She was booked on the evening Iberia flight to Heathrow and had one carry-on.

She turned to him before heading to security and said, 'I'll text you when I get home. Please take care, Jack.'

She leaned forward to kiss him on the cheek but he turned his head quickly and she kissed him full on the lips. They held each other tightly and to anyone looking on nearby, they were two lovers parting at an airport.

'I'm going to miss you, Jack. I know you've been working but I've loved being here with you.'

He whispered, 'I'll get back as soon as I can. Call me when you land. I wish you weren't going but it's for the best. I'm going to miss you too.'

Eva took hold of the handle of her carry-on and walked away looking back before disappearing into the crowd and making for security.

***

As he drove back into Malaga, Jack thought of Eva. She was wonderful company and great to look at. He also knew he'd one less worry on his hands. Over the next few days he was going to dig deep into the affairs of Vicente. He had no idea of the size of the organisation he was up against but his first visit would be to Juan's paint shop, and he took a diversion to the garage. As he drove past it he noticed a blue Seat Ibiza for sale in the front. The sign on the windscreen said 1995 euros. Jack smiled to himself and muttered, 'Perfect, I'll be there in the morning.'

It was 10.00 next morning when Jack pulled into the front of Juan's garage and he turned the car around with the bonnet facing towards the street. Old habits. He sauntered across to the Seat and started walking round it. Juan arrived after a couple of minutes.

'Nice, isn't it?'

'It looks okay. Can I see inside?'

'Sure.' Juan had the keys in his hand and Jack heard the click as he unlocked the doors.

Feigning acute interest, Jack began examining the interior.

'It's for my daughter so I need to be sure it's okay. Do you have a service record for it?'

'It's in the office with the rest of the documents. Have a good look round the car then just come over.'

Jack could see the car had been cleaned up for potential buyers and for good measure he looked under the bonnet and checked the engine.

He walked over to the office and the smell of paint hit him as he entered. 'Looks pretty good. Can I see the documents?'

Juan began searching through a drawer in his desk and pulled out a buff-coloured folder. As he did so Jack looked out of the window of the office and saw the back of a black Audi A7 sticking out of a lock-up at the back of the yard. He knew from the registration it was Vicente's.

Juan brought out a sheaf of papers from the file and placed them on the table. 'Here we are.'

Jack looked at the service history and saw several gaps and a couple of blurred stamps. 'So how many owners has it had?'

'Three according to the records.'

Jack knew it was bullshit. 'It looks as if it could be what I'm looking for.' Then he nodded at the A7 outside. 'I'm looking for myself as well. I need a 4 x 4 for a couple of trips to Switzerland and I'm in a hurry.' He kept a straight face as Juan looked at him intently.

'Are you serious?'

'Yeah, of course. It's the sort of vehicle I need.'

' Just give me a minute. I need to make a phone call.'

Juan left the office and went into the paint shop. Jack saw him turn away and speak into his phone. He quickly turned round the oil-smudged diary on the desk in front of him and photographed as many pages as he could. He pretended to be checking his phone as Juan came back.

'Maybe I can help you. Can you give me a contact number?'

'Sure.' Jack gave him his mobile number. It had risks but he now had a connection.

Juan put Jack's number into his phone and said, 'The Audi owner isn't around at the moment but he should be here in a few days. I'll let you know. So how about the Seat?'

'Let me talk to my daughter and get back to you.' He knew Juan didn't believe him.

Later in his room he studied the images he'd grabbed from Juan's desk diary. There didn't seem to be much of interest but there was a number scribbled on one of the pages. It caught his attention because he recognised it as a London number. He wrote it down in his book. He'd ring it in the morning rather than risk leaving a message.

It was the evening now and still hot. Jack needed a walk and left the hotel to stroll around the Old Town. It wouldn't be the same without Eva and he suddenly realised how much he missed her.

***

Vicente was in a bar in Puerto Banús when Juan called him.

'Don't want to bother you but some guy wants to buy your Audi.'

'How does he know it's for sale?'

'He doesn't. He came in to look at a Seat I have on the front. Saw your vehicle and asked if it was for sale.'

'You were supposed to keep it fucking hidden.'

'The garage door was open. It's fucking hot as if you didn't know.'

Vicente said, 'Okay calm down. This could help me. Who's the guy?'

'Some Brit. Looking for a 4 x 4 to get him to Switzerland and back. It'll be cash he said. He's in a hurry.'

'Okay. Find out the current value for me and give the Audi a valet. I'll give you a call later.'

'I'm on it. I got his registration number. It's a hire car but I've got a few contacts. Shouldn't be too difficult to find his name.'

'Okay, that would be useful. Let's make sure he's legit.'

Vicente ended the call and glanced around the bar. Everyone looked carefree and happy. All he could see was a gathering train wreck for him. He finished his drink and paid his bar bill. His Puerto Banús pied-à-terre was under half a mile away and he'd shower before hitting the clubs. He needed some distraction, some female company. When he got inside his car he rang Frank.

'Any news?'

'Nothing. Not a fucking thing.'

Vicente shouted, 'I don't believe this.'

'Me neither. Where are you?'

'It doesn't matter where the fuck I am. Some bastard has the shipment. Call me when you hear anything.'

***

Rico phoned Vicente at 8pm exactly. Vicente saw the caller ID and let it ring. The voice message said, 'Call me now.' He took a large swallow of his Soberano and went for his shower. His taxi arrived at 10pm and he asked for Dreams nightclub. Walking past the queue he was guided inside by security and he headed straight for the bar and asked for a bottle of Veuve Clicquot. He nodded towards a table next to a party of girls.

'It will be right over, sir.'

Vicente bought three more bottles as the night wore on and at 1.30am he took out his wallet and selected a black credit card with no limit. He invited two girls back to his place. Within fifteen minutes they all tumbled into his bed and the girls took it in turn to pleasure him. With all the booze he'd consumed, he kept getting their names mixed up before forgetting them altogether. He eventually fell asleep at 4am.

He woke up six hours later and found himself alone. His head was pounding and his phone was ringing. By the time he focused, he'd missed the call. He hit voicemail and heard Rico's voice.

'I'm on my way over.'

He threw back the sheets and slowly got to his feet. His head reeled as he stood up and he made it to the shower, where he turned on the water and took a piss at the same time.

He rang Juan after he finished getting dressed and said, 'Sell the Audi. Just get as near to the value as you can.'

'I don't have the documents.'

'I'll worry about that. Just get back to the guy and say I'll call him about sending the documents on to him.'

'Okay, I'll sort that out now. Just before you go, Rico has been calling me and wants to know where you are. He sounded really pissed.'

'Best you don't know, Juan, but the way things are I need some cash fast. Call me when you have a deal on the vehicle. If Rico calls again don't tell him I'm selling the Audi.' Vicente ended the call and lit up a Marlborough.

***

Frank had given Salvador the directions on where to meet him. The lock-up garage was in Hackney in south London underneath the railway lines and the floor shook as a train passed overhead every few minutes. It took Salvador ten minutes to extract the package from the driver's mirror and the same for the other one. Within half an hour both mirrors were back looking as before. Frank placed both packages on a table next to the car and opened a drawer in the desk next to him. Taking out a small set of scales he checked the seals on the bags and weighed them. Both were exactly half a kilo.

'You don't think I opened them do you, Frank?'

'No, because you wouldn't be here if you did.'

'Meaning?'

'You'd be fucking dead. This stuff is lethal. Just need to sniff a bag of fentanyl and it's curtains.'

Salvador placed his tools in the back of the car and straightened up. 'So what happens now?'

'You'll be paid in the next couple of days. Fifty thousand euros as agreed. We need to get this stuff distributed and as soon as we get paid, you get paid. What you do with your cut and where you go is up to you but I'd avoid Malaga for a while. Forever, probably. I've arranged a hotel for you near Kings Cross. Give me forty-eight hours then come back for your money.' Frank handed him five hundred pounds in twenties. 'That's a cash advance to keep you going in London. Remember you're here on holiday. I'll see you in two days. Leave the car and we'll fix the mirrors.'

Salvador pocketed the money and began walking towards the door. He looked at the car and said, 'How much is all that stuff worth?'

'It could kill half of London. You tell me.'

Salvador sauntered off and looked for a taxi.

Chapter Seventeen

The café was within sight of Marble Arch and the young couple drinking their lattes seemed in high spirits. Tony finished his drink and looked around before leaning towards Rebecca. 'I'm told we have some lovely stuff coming in this week. Top grade and just in time for Saturday night. Is the party still on?'

Rebecca spooned the last of the milk from her drink and said, 'Of course. It'll be brilliant. There should be around a dozen coming plus a few hangers-on hoping for a hit. When will you get the stuff?'

'Probably Friday night or Saturday morning. My supplier has changed for this one but I've been told it will be the best.'

Rebecca grinned and said, 'If it's Friday night we could test it out.'

'I'll press for Friday.' Tony leaned across and kissed her just as his mobile rang. He took the call and spoke only to say, 'Okay that's good. I'll wait to hear from you.'

Rebecca waited until he finished the call. 'And?'

'It's in. We should be able to have some fun on Friday night. He'll call back with a time and place to meet up. I need to sort out the money.'

Rebecca pushed back her chair and laughed. 'Can't wait.'

***

Jack woke to a beautiful blue Malaga sky and showered before going down to breakfast. The staff knew him now and he was greeted warmly by the waitress.

'*Buen dia*, Jack.'

He replied in his best Spanish, ordered a pot of coffee and walked across to the self-service buffet. Back at his table he placed his plate of scrambled eggs on his mat and checked his phone for messages. There was only one and it was from Eva. '*Buen dia*, Jack.' He smiled. Second time in five minutes. 'I hope you slept well. I didn't. Phone me today if you can.' She had added a little kiss at the end. He would call her later.

Finishing breakfast, he returned to his room and sat on the bed before taking his pay-as–you-go phone from his bag. He was going to assume a drugs connection and phoned the number he'd found scribbled in Juan's diary. He waited and was about to end the call when a male voice answered, 'Hello.'

'Hi, it's Len.'

'Who the fuck is Len?'

'I'm a friend of Juan. He asked me to call about buying some gear.'

'What gear?'

'He said you'd know.'

'Fuck you.'

The line went dead and Jack ended the call on his phone. He hadn't expected to learn much, but he'd find the location from the phone number and pay a visit on his return to the UK. This was his best London connection to Susan as the options began running out in Spain.

***

Two miles away in the east side of Malaga, Juan made a call to an old friend Sergio.

'It's Juan. How are you my friend?'

'Okay, what are you after?'

'I need a name of a renter from Marcar.'

'Is that all? What's in it for me?'

'The usual dinner for you and your family at your favourite restaurant and a taxi home.'

'Okay. Give me the registration and make and I'll call you back.'

He phoned back in ten minutes. 'Your renter is a Mr Jack Barclay. Lives in London.'

'Do you have his address there?'

'No, but I have a Spanish one. He's staying at the Hotel Carmen here in Malaga.'

'Thank you. Good work, Sergio. Just let me know when you want your big night out.'

'Don't worry, I will.'

Vicente picked up Juan's call on the first ring.

'I've got the name of the guy who wants to buy your Audi. He's from London but is staying at the Hotel Carmen in Malaga. His name is Jack Barclay.'

'I'll check him out. Have you heard anything from Salvador?'

'Nothing. He's fucking disappeared.'

'Bastard. Call me anytime if you hear anything.'

'I will.'

Vicente was agitated and Googled Jack Barclay, London and at first found details of a luxury motor car outlet in west London. He kept scrolling and then found what he was looking for. A private investigator. He wrote down the contact details. There was no address. He leant back in his chair. 'Fuck.'

He rang Juan back. 'The guy who wants to buy my Audi. Tell him I'll meet him at Café El Barco tomorrow at 10am. I'll be sitting by the window.'

'What if he can't make it?'

'He either wants it or he doesn't.'

' I'll tell him.'

Vicente heard back from Juan in half an hour. 'He'll meet you at 10am. He wants to see the documents first then inspect the vehicle.'

'I'll have all that with me.'

***

Eva picked up Jack's call quickly.

'I'm meeting with Vicente at 10.00 tomorrow morning. I wanted you to know.'

'Where are you meeting him?'

'At a café in Malaga called El Barco. It was his choice.'

'What are you going to say to him?'

'I'll confront him.'

'Will you ask about Susan?'

'Yes. It's a public place and there's only so much he can do. It's the only way to move all this along now. If I can't get anything out of him then I'll catch a flight to London tomorrow night. There's nothing much for me to look at in Malaga now.'

'I wish you were here now. Will you call me after you've seen him?'

'Of course. Goodnight, Eva.'

'Night, Jack.'

***

Vicente rose at 7am and showered. He'd leave Puerto Banús at 8.00 for his meeting at El Barco. He wanted to be there first and watch Jack Barclay arrive. He folded the documents for the Audi and placed them inside his laptop case. Choosing a beige cotton jacket and trousers, he finished dressing and percolated some coffee. As he poured it, his mobile rang. It was Rico and he let it go to message. He took a large gulp of coffee and left his apartment.

He found a parking place about two hundred metres away and checked his watch. 9.40. He walked towards El Barco and as he approached, he saw a man sitting in the window seat. The man stood as he entered and extended his hand. 'Jack Barclay.'

Vicente knew he'd lost the initiative and ignored the outstretched hand. 'You're early.'

'It's a nice morning. The light woke me.'

Vicente sat down as the waitress appeared. 'Just a black coffee.' As she moved to the next table he said, 'I hear you want to buy my Audi.'

'I couldn't care less about your Audi. I think you know why I want to speak to you.'

Vicente took his Marlborough pack from his pocket and said, 'Let's sit outside.' He nodded to the waitress that they were going to sit out and she nodded back.

Vicente held his lighter under the end of the cigarette and inhaled deeply. 'What the fuck are you talking about? I came here to sell my vehicle. Nothing more.'

Jack waited before saying, 'Why did Susan die?'

'Who's Susan?'

'I know who you are,' Jack replied, 'and what you do.'

'Do you now? Well of course you're a hot shot private detective. You know everything, eh?'

Jack ignored the jibe and went on, 'You're right about my occupation. The trail has led from London to you and you have big problems now.'

'What the fuck is that supposed to mean?'

'You're in trouble. Money has gone missing.'

Vicente leaned back as the waitress arrived and he took another drag from his cigarette. He asked, 'What do you know about that?'

Jack heard the surprise in Vicente's voice and sensed he might just have hit a nerve. He bluffed and said, 'You have people after you.'

'Doesn't everyone. Anyway, I don't know who the fuck you are. Could be a cop for all I know?'

'I'm no cop but you've got a big problem and I've got a client who wants to know why Susan Long died. There are people looking for you. Nobody's looking for me. I would be happy if I never saw you again, but maybe we can help each other.'

Vicente stubbed his cigarette out and sipped the last of his coffee. He put his cup down and looked at Jack. 'Go fuck yourself.' He kicked his chair back and got up from the table.

Jack remained seated. 'Please yourself, Vicente. So, you don't want to know where the lost money is at Susan's villa?'

Vicente hesitated but kept walking.

'See you around,' Jack called after him. 'Your choice.'

He took out his wallet and paid the bill, leaving a tip.

Chapter Eighteen

Salvador was feeling good. He had lots of cash in his pocket and London was buzzing. He'd laid low on his first night to recover from the drive, but he would hit the town tonight and have some fun. Tomorrow he'd be a rich man. He'd already decided to head to Ibiza after his pay out. He'd use cash for the first couple of months until the heat died down. The other islands were a short ferry journey away and he'd just keep on the move if he had to. He showered and checked himself in the mirror then took the lift down to the hotel bar for a drink. It was only 8pm and he would hit the clubs later.

The Spanish brandy tasted good and reminded him of nights in Malaga. After his second drink the barman sidled up. 'You looking for anything special tonight, sir?'

Salvador gave a shrug of his shoulders. 'What you got in mind?'

'I can get a very beautiful lady for you. Make your London visit memorable. European, Asian, English. Any country you choose.'

'Okay. Spanish.'

The barman nodded. 'Give me time to make a call. I'll be back.'

Salvador drank slowly and thought of female company for the night. He saw another barman take over, then the one who spoke to him returned.

'I think you will be very pleased. I have exactly the type of girl you want. Just fifty pounds to me and it's all fixed.'

'How do you know what I like? Go fuck yourself.'

He rose from his bar stool and tipped his glass over the bar top. As the last of his drink sprayed over the barman's trousers, he made his finger and thumb like a gun and pointed it towards the man before he got up and left.

He jumped in a taxi and asked the driver for a good Spanish night club. Twenty minutes later they pulled up outside a building in a side street near Charing Cross. The club was subterranean and dark and the music was smooth. He took a stool at the bar and ordered a brandy. He relaxed and took in the atmosphere. Life was good. The girl he asked to dance was from Valencia and by 1am the odour of sweat and alcohol clung to them as they moved slowly in the centre of the floor. By 3am they were in Salvador's room in King's Cross.

She rolled over and prodded him at 7am. 'I don't know how I'll do it but I have to go to work.'

Salvador grunted and looked up. 'Hasta la vista. See you in Valencia.'

She dressed quickly and let herself out.

***

Salvador slept on until 9.00 and awoke to the sound of sirens. Looking out of the window he saw two fire engines passing at speed and he opened the blind to let the light in. Then everything sunk in. The night he'd spent with the cute Spanish girl and the headache he had from too many cigarettes and too much brandy. He showered and felt better for it before going downstairs for breakfast. As he began to focus on his surroundings he chose from the hot buffet.

Today he would have real money in his hands. His small case took minutes to pack and he was told at reception he had nothing to pay. Taxis were scarce but he flagged one down after a few minutes and asked for Hackney.

'What's the address, guv?'

'I'll tell you when we get there.'

He paid off the taxi when he recognised the surroundings and walked towards the lock-up. Turning the corner, he spotted the archway where he had met Frank and was surprised to see the graffiti-scrawled shutters locked, with no sign of life. He walked up and tested the doors then knocked loudly. He turned as he heard somebody behind him.

'Looking for something?'

'Yeah, where's the guy who worked out of here?'

'I'm just across from him. Never knew him. He locked up yesterday and drove off. Last I've seen of him.'

Salvador froze then kicked the lock-up door.

'You okay, mate?'

He cursed under his breath and walked away.

Chapter Nineteen

Rico left his home in Tarifa at 5am and drove north on the E15 towards Malaga. Vicente was a key player in the organisation but he knew there was a big problem now. The silence told him the fentanyl shipment was in trouble. Rico had always managed to stay at arm's length from his opiate trading and his pals at the golf club just thought his import business in outdoor rattan furniture was extremely successful. Vicente had told him the missing payment on the previous deal was forthcoming but he'd heard nothing. He knew where to find him in Puerto Banús even though Vicente thought it was his secret hide-away, and his journey would take less than an hour at this time of the morning. He tried to contain his anger and reduced his speed to stay inside the limit.

The dawn sky had changed from bright yellow to a giant ball of orange as he approached his destination and he stopped one street short of Vicente's place and parked. The knife he brought was of the old variety but he liked it. One press of the button and the six-inch blade flicked out. He pushed it into his inside pocket and climbed out of his car.

Apart from a couple of cats creeping out of narrow alleyways there was no one to see him and he made his way to the small house at the end of the street. He saw no sign of life inside and jumped up on the perimeter wall and into the back yard. Bringing out his knife he slipped the blade into the patio door lock and heard a click. Sliding the door open just enough to step inside he found himself in what appeared to be a small living room. He kept his knife in his left hand and made his way towards a door on his right.

The morning sun was beginning to penetrate the interior and he saw the flight of stairs ahead of him. He made his way up towards two closed doors at the top. The one on the right was slightly wider and he took it to be the bedroom door. Taking hold of the handle he eased the door open and let his eyes become accustomed to the semi darkness. He saw the outline of two people on the king size bed and went over to the snoring side. A white sheet barely covered Vicente, who was lying on his back, and a young-looking dark-haired woman curled up next to him.

Rico punched him hard in the groin and Vicente screamed out in pain. 'What the fuck.' The woman shouted and jumped out of the other side of the bed. Rico saw her naked back as she ran to a chair and grabbed her clothes before making for the door.

Vicente managed to raise his head. 'What the fuck are you doing?'

Rico heard the door slam as the girl ran for safety. He hauled Vicente out of the bed and pushed him onto the chair and towered over him. 'Right, bring me up to date. Where's the missing money from the last consignment and where's the fentanyl?'

Vicente started talking at break neck speed. 'I can get the money from the cocaine deal. There was a misunderstanding along the line.' He started to stand up.

Rico pushed him back into the chair and rasped, 'What do you mean a misunderstanding?'

'The money was hidden for safety but I know how to find it.'

'You were in charge, Vicente.'

'I know, but it's complicated.'

'Don't fucking tell me about complications.' Rico took a step back and punched Vicente straight on the mouth. 'The money. Where is it?'

'It's here in Malaga. I stashed it at Susan's house for safety but it's been moved.'

'What do you mean moved?'

Vicente wiped the blood from the side of his mouth. 'It's safe. I know how to find it. You'll have it in two days. I promise you.'

'You've got twenty-four hours. No more. Now where's the fentanyl?'

'We've lost contact with Salvador. Maybe something's gone wrong with his phone. We should be able to contact him today.'

Rico balled his fist and punched Vicente straight in the gut. 'If you spent less time sleeping around and more time looking after the business you might know what's going on. I want the money from the previous shipment and I want to know the fentanyl has reached its destination.' He took out the knife and flicked the blade before scraping it across Vicente's throat. Blood from the cut trickled down the side of his neck. 'It will be a pleasure to do it ear to ear next time and believe me I'll find you or one of your family. Twenty-four hours. That's all.'

Rico took hold of him by the shoulders and threw him onto the floor. before walking out and slamming the door behind him.

Chapter Twenty

Jack took the call in his room at the Carmen.

'It's Vicente. I need to see you today.'

'You know where I am. Why don't you come here? There's a good café just down the street.'

'How about 10am?'

'That's good. See you in reception.'

Jack put the phone back on its receiver and walked over to the window in his small room. As he looked out on the early morning comings and goings of life around him he began to think of Eva and wished she was here. He knew he was going to make Vicente talk today but he also knew the dangers. He texted Eva. 'Big day today and hope to make progress. Will call you tonight. Best, Jack x.'

His phone bleeped within a minute. The text said, 'Please take care of yourself. Call when you can xx.'

At 9.45 Jack exited the hotel and walked across the road to a café and chose an outside table back from the road. He ordered a white coffee and waited. At 9.55 a taxi pulled up and Vicente stepped out. He was on his own and looked around before entering the Carmen. Jack left his money on the table and waited another minute before getting up and walking across the road. Vicente was sitting at a table near reception.

Jack walked up to him and noticed a plaster on the side of his neck and the bruising on his face and mouth. 'You look as if you didn't sleep too well.'

Vicente grunted and winced as he rose from his padded chair. 'We need to talk.'

'Do we?'

'Let's go for a walk. I think we can help each other.'

'The only way you can help me is to tell me about the death of Susan Long. That's why I'm here.'

'Let's get out of here, Mr Barclay. I have things to say to you.'

They made their way to the front door and out into the warm morning sunlight. Jack pointed left and they came to a café with outside tables shaded by plane trees. They both asked for a white coffee and the waiter left.

'So, what do you have for me, Vicente?'

'I want to do a deal.'

Jack shrugged. 'Go on.'

'You said you know where the money is at Susan's place. You tell me where and I'll tell you what I know about her death.'

Jack waited as the waiter returned then said, 'I suspect you are in considerable danger. My part of the deal is provable, yours isn't. You tell me your story then I'll decide whether to help you.'

Vicente grimaced before taking a sip of his coffee. 'What makes you think I'm in danger. What do you know?'

'Missing drugs money is never forgotten. You'll be hunted until you're found.'

Vicente lit up a cigarette. 'I've got twenty-four hours to pass the money over. If I don't then you won't find me. I'll tell you what I know, but remember your part of the deal. You can be hunted too.' He took a large pull on his cigarette and went on, 'Susan was a courier for us. She didn't need to be but she wanted money to pay off business debts. She knew the risks but unknown to us she became a user herself. Cocaine was her thing and when she was in London she couldn't wait to party. She loved the life and everyone loved her. The trouble was it was our cocaine she was skimming, both to use and to sell. When I found out, I warned her but she was too much into the habit. At first the amounts were small but of course she became complacent. We started to get complaints about the purity and we knew somebody was diluting it with God knows what. It all came to a head at a party last month when Susan was high. She told someone how easy it was for her to access as much as she needed. That person told someone else and before we knew it the whole operation was compromised. It was decided she was too dangerous to keep on. She began to make threats in order to keep her business and her lifestyle, not to mention her habit. Had she just walked away and kept quiet she could well be alive today. I had nothing to do with her death and you must believe that. In fact, I didn't know she was dead until after it had happened.' He paused and said, 'We had a close relationship.'

Jack stopped him there. 'So, who arranged her death?'

'How would I know? She was asked to be in a certain place in London at a certain time and she agreed to that. Her journey must have been monitored and as she drove through west London somebody flagged her into the side of the road. Then a guy flew out of the hotel window. I'm told he was alive when he fell, but drugged up.' He added, 'Wrong place wrong time for both of them.'

Jack shot a glance at him and said, 'I want you to know three things. I'm only here talking to you because I need information. The second thing is that I despise you and everyone else like you who is involved in drug trafficking.'

Vicente asked, 'What's the third?'

'I don't believe you weren't involved in Susan's death.'

'You asked me to tell you what I know about Susan and I've told you.'

Jack pushed him again. 'You've told me a little, but it's not my life on the line. With Susan gone, who has taken her place? You must still be making the runs to the UK.'

Vicente's facial expression tightened. 'You have what you wanted, now talk to me.'

'If only life was that easy, eh, Vicente. If I walk away right now, you're dead and I need some more. It's up to you.'

Vicente made to get up then sat down. 'What are you after?'

'Some information on the organisation.'

Vicente put his hands out palm first. 'No way I can give you that.'

Jack threw a ten-euro note on the table for the coffees and got up.

Vicente looked up at him and waved his hand to tell him to sit back down.

'The stuff goes by road through Dover. The last planned consignment would have gone through yesterday in a black Audi 6 with Spanish plates. The P&O ferry cameras will tell you the rest about the car and its driver. You can track it into London from Dover. Okay, Mr Barclay that information can't be traced back to me and I'm not saying any more. Now it's your turn.'

Jack guessed the information he'd just given wasn't necessarily correct but knew it was pretty much all he was going to get. He noticed a slight twitch in Vicente's left hand as he spoke and waited in the hope of more.

Vicente leaned forward and said, 'Some people know the business I'm in and it was safer to keep the money at Susan's villa. It isn't where I hid it so where did she move it to?'

Jack gave him the hiding place at the swimming pool and Vicente stood up, turned his back and left.

***

Jack went back to his room and hung the 'Do Not Disturb' sign on his door. Sitting on the bed he rang his contact at Malaga Police.

'It's Jack Barclay. We need to speak either in person or on a secure phone.'

The male voice said, 'Ring me on this number.'

Jack wrote down a mobile number and re-dialled.

The voice asked, 'What have you got for me?'

Jack told him of his meeting with Vicente, his complicity in Susan's murder and the route by which the drugs were being trafficked to the UK along with the vehicle involved in the latest run.

'He wouldn't give me any more. His life is in danger now because of the missing drug money and he will probably make an attempt to retrieve it from the swimming pool at Susan's in the next twenty-four hours.'

'Did you tell him where it was?'

'I had to trade something to get information on Susan's death and the method being used to move the drugs from Spain to the UK.'

There was a silence then the voice said, 'Okay, we'll be waiting for him. Did he say anything about the supply chain here in Malaga?'

'No. He wasn't going to say any more than he did, but surely his arrest is going to worry the organisation.'

'We can make some progress from here. Best we keep this to ourselves for the moment. I'm just going to refer to you as a source. I'll call you with any updates. Are you still in Malaga?'

'Yes, at the Hotel Carmen.'

Chapter Twenty-One

The night air was still hot and the moon was hidden by cloud. Perfect for Vicente as he parked down the street from Susan's home. He waited for half an hour and watched but saw no light or activity nearby. At 1am he killed the dome light and quietly opened the door of his vehicle. Nudging it shut, he didn't hit the lock remote on his key and walked towards Susan's with a black rucksack on his back. He turned down the side track and worked his way round to the rear wall of her garden and waited. Only the gentle sound of the surf and distant barking of dogs broke the silence and he crouched down as the moon appeared through some broken high cloud. In five minutes the darkness returned and he stood then jumped up to look over the top. He could see the darkened villa behind the covered swimming pool and hauled himself up before dropping down on the other side. He made his way to the life-saving ring on the other side of the pool and pulled off the rucksack. Pulling out a knife and a small torch he began cutting at the seam running along the middle of the ring. As the threads began to separate, his sawing motion became more intense. He ripped open the fabric and his hand felt something spongy inside. Plunging his hand in, he pulled out a wad of coloured paper. His fingers kept ripping the paper out and suddenly he was bathed in a sea of intense light. The voice barked from behind the barbeque, 'Police, don't move and get down on the ground now.' Vicente heard the sound of guns being cocked and sank to his knees. His only thought was, *Fuck you, Jack Barclay.*

***

'Eva, it's Jack.'

'Jack. How are you?'

'I'm fine. It's been a busy kind of a day and I have an update for you. I would rather speak to you face to face because I have found out about events leading up to Susan's death. It's not quite what you hoped or expected but I'll tell you over the phone if you would like to know now.'

'Yes, please tell me now.'

'Okay, if you're sure.' He hesitated before saying, 'Susan was not living the life you thought. It looks as if she was using cocaine and in fact, she was bringing consignments into London from Spain on a regular basis.'

Eva gasped and several moments passed before she spoke. 'Oh, my God, no. Then she was murdered?'

'I would say everything points to her having been murdered, but I don't have proof yet. She got mixed up with a class A drug smuggling cartel and obviously there was huge money involved. They're still trafficking into the UK and I'm in contact with the police here in Malaga. I'm really sorry to tell you this.'

'How did you find out?'

'From Vicente and I've no reason to disbelieve him. He wouldn't tell me more. I'll be here for the next two days to dig around. I'll call you soon.'

'This is all a bit of a shock,' Eva replied, 'and I need some time for it to sink in. I would never have guessed any of this about my sister. We need to meet up as soon as you get back. I'm seeing an old girlfriend for a drink tonight but my phone will be on. Call if you want to.'

'I may well just do that. Speak later.'

'Bye, Jack.'

Chapter Twenty-Two

It was 10am and Rico was on a lounger watching his pool man clear the overnight insects from the water when a call came. The voice sounded nervous and he recognised it as his snitch, connected to the local police.

'Vicente has been arrested. A guy called Jack Barclay has been mentioned.'

'Who's he?'

'A Private Investigator from London.'

Rico stubbed his cigarette out in the ashtray next to his lounger and picked up his phone. 'Book me on Iberia to London tonight. I'll stay at my usual hotel.'

The voice replied, 'Yes of course. I'll call you back to confirm flight times.'

Rico placed the phone back on the table next to him and pushed his hand through his thick black hair. He had to find the fentanyl or lose everything he'd worked for. The London detective would return home after delving into other people's business in Malaga and he would find out what he knew. After that, he would be surplus to requirements.

Shrugging off his robe he set the stopwatch on his wrist and told the pool man to clear off for the day. Diving naked into the pool, he began his morning regime of fifty lengths, determined to shave a few seconds off yesterday's time.

***

Tony left his desk and walked outside. It was late Friday afternoon in Shoreditch and by the look of the traffic, the London weekend exodus had already started. He hit his supplier's number and waited. The voice said, 'Hello.'

'It's me, Tony. You said you'd call. Can we meet up? I need some stuff for tonight.'

'Sure, be in the car park of the Dog and Duck just off the top of City Road. Let's say seven o'clock. It'll cost a bit more. This is the very best. What are you driving?'

'I'll be in a blue Kuga.'

'Okay, see you at seven.'

He called Rebecca. 'Can you speak?'

'Just give me a second. What's up?'

'I'll have the stuff for tonight.'

Rebecca squealed, 'Great, I've had a shit day and need some fun. Why don't you come round about eight. I'll get a takeaway and I've got some booze.'

'Brilliant. See you at eight on the dot.' They both laughed and finished the call.

As he walked back into the office he thought of the night to come with her. He fired off a couple of emails to get the last of the work off his desk and closed down his laptop. There were no more meetings scheduled and without saying anything, he hung his jacket over his arm and sauntered out. He'd stop off at the Prince Albert for a couple of pints before carrying on to meet his contact and buy the party rations. It was going to be some weekend.

***

After Tony's call, Frank got busy. He only had a gram of heavily cut cocaine left so he ground up some baking soda and added benzocaine. It still looked small so he finely crushed two paracetamol tablets and mixed it all together using a couple of spoons. Wrapping a kitchen towel round his face, he opened the pack of fentanyl and extracted an amount with one of the spoons. This would give them the hit they were looking for. He added this to the pile of white crystals in front of him and mashed everything together. Using his scales he weighed out three grams and tipped it all into a clear plastic bag. He had half a gram left over and knew he could sell it in any pub. Removing the towel from his face he cleared up, washing the chopping board and spoons before retreating into his living room to watch television. He felt good at the thought of making some money again.

***

Salvador had rung Frank again and there was still no response. It was the only number he had for him and didn't know his address. He was back in his hotel room and lay on the bed, chain-smoking. The intermittent night siren sounds of London crept through the window and he became angrier as the minutes passed. As his fury increased, he stubbed out his cigarette and reached for his phone.

He wasn't going to be the fall-guy for this and rang a number he had never used before.

'Rico, it's Salvador.'

The voice snarled, 'The missing driver, eh! Where the fuck are you?'

'In London. Frank has gone.'

'Where's the stuff? Where's the fucking stuff?'

'I don't know. I only delivered it.'

Rico shouted, 'Vicente said he'd lost track of you.'

Salvador kept calm and replied, 'Frank was calling the shots I just thought there had been some security issues. I don't know what Frank is up to.'

'Stay where you are. I'm on my way to London tonight. Where are you staying?'

'I'm at the Marquis in Kings Cross.'

'I'll meet up with you in the morning.'

Salvador stood and packed his overnight case before checking the room and bathroom to make sure he left nothing behind. As he walked through the lobby he saw there was only one man behind the check-in desk and he was dealing with a young lady who seemed to be making a fuss about her bill. Salvador left through the front door and turned left towards St. Pancras. He'd take the Eurostar to Paris and be back in Spain in twenty-four hours, but would give Malaga a miss for a long time. At least he was alive.

***

Vicente sat brooding in his cell and weighed up the odds. He'd been caught red-handed trying to retrieve over a hundred thousand euros of drug money. He could say he didn't know it was drug money but his relationship with Susan and the villa wouldn't help. A little police work would unearth all his connections and they had his mobile phone. He was due for another interview with the detectives in an hour and he had to decide whether to stonewall them or give them some information. At the very least he would start to get his revenge against the private detective.

The interview room was small and had no air conditioning or if it did they'd switched it off. Vicente was refused a cigarette and the voice recorder was activated with the date and time being given together with the names of the participants.

Before they had a chance to ask their first question Vicente said, 'I can maybe help you, but I want a deal.' The weary-looking lead detective pushed his hand through his greying hair and leaned back on his chair. 'I can't promise you anything, but tell us what you know and we'll take it from there.'

Vicente asked again for a cigarette and was given one. 'I've got information that will open this whole thing up for you. But I'll need protection and I don't mean going to prison.'

'What are we talking about here, Vicente?'

'We're talking a kilo of fentanyl, worth up to a million on the streets when cut into bad cocaine and probably hundreds of deaths. Oh, and I'm told there's a girl with the private detective. Maybe you should take a look at her.' Vicente smiled to himself as he planted the first lie.

The silence lasted a few seconds then the detective said, 'Are you talking about Susan's sister?'

Vicente paused and decided to bluff it. 'Yeah that's her. Who knows why she's really here.'

Vicente was on a roll and was enjoying spinning his tale to the small audience.

The detective sitting across from him made some notes and said, 'Okay, what's your part in all this?'

Vicente said, 'I don't feel too good. Must be the heat. I need a break.'

The recorder was switched off as Vicente sat back and exhaled a long plume of smoke before stubbing the cigarette out in the ashtray in front of him. He stood up to be taken back to his cell, but he felt good at the thought of the damage he'd just done to Jack Barclay. He was regaining some control. He had to make a deal.

***

Jack was determined to find those behind Susan's assassination and needed more news for Eva. Questions had stuck in his mind throughout the investigation. Why the barbarity? Was there more to know about Susan's role inside the organisation? He wondered if she really had been the intended target. With Vicente in custody and no more news following his arrest, Jack knew there was little more he could achieve in Malaga and booked a flight to London. He only had two things to go on. The London phone number he found scribbled on Juan's desk diary at the paint shop and the whereabouts of the black Audi that passed through the Port of Dover. It wasn't a lot but he'd worked with less in the past.

His flight to London Gatwick left on time and he dozed off in his window seat as the plane settled into its cruising altitude. He knew he'd soon miss the warm evenings of southern Spain but the thought of meeting Eva helped dismiss any negative thoughts about the weather. He texted her as he travelled into London on the Gatwick Express. 'Hi Eva. Back in UK and on train to London. I should be home around 7pm. Will call you tonight.'

His phoned chimed in a couple of minutes and all the message said was, 'Yes. Can we meet up?'

His reply was, 'Of course. Yours or mine?'

'Mine. I'll cook. Bring wine.'

'Should be with you about 8.30pm.'

All he received in reply was 'X'.

***

He was home just after 7pm and checked the messages on his land line as he waited for the water to heat up. There was nothing of any consequence and he showered and changed into a fresh white shirt and jeans before picking out a bottle of three-year-old Rioja from his wine rack. He hoped it would be as good as the one they had shared three nights before.

In half an hour he was on his way to the Tube station for the dash across London. The worst of the evening commute was over and the crowds were thinning. He tapped
on Eva's door in Clapham just before 8.30.

She was wearing a loose-fitting white blouse and a blue skirt and leaned forward and kissed him. As she shut the door and led the way in, she turned and said, 'I thought you would like a Spanish dish tonight. We'll have to create our own heat, Jack.'

They walked into the small dining room and he laughed as he placed the bottle on the candle-lit table. He listened to the Spanish guitar classical music playing in the background and said, 'It's nice to be back in Andalucía.'

Eva touched his arm as she went to pick up the bottle. 'I'm looking forward to that glass of red. There's a corkscrew on the side dresser. I won't be a moment.'

Jack watched her as she walked into the kitchen and he began opening the wine. She returned with a terracotta casserole dish in her gloved hands and placed it in the middle of the table.

Sitting down, they clinked glasses and Jack said, 'I missed you after you left Malaga.'

'I missed you when I returned to London. Maybe we should make up for lost time?'

'Yes, I think so. Malaga wasn't the same without you.'

Eva gave him a peck on the cheek and said, 'Let's eat. I'm starving.'

She had cooked chicken in a red wine sauce with rice on the side. 'There's some garlic in this, Jack so we have to eat equal amounts. No cheating.'

Jack didn't talk about Susan, only because he was enjoying their time together. 'I can't remember being quite so relaxed, Eva. Must be the wine.'

Eva gently kicked him under the table and he leaned across and kissed her.

'Shall we skip dessert?'

Eva nodded and they both got up from the table. Jack took her into a close hold and they danced slowly to the music. He couldn't remember feeling so happy and as she rested her head on his shoulder he heard her whisper, 'Let's go, Jack.'

Without a word, they walked through to the only bedroom and as they kissed, their hands began moving over each other's bodies. They began undressing each other and fell onto the bed.

***

Rico landed at Heathrow and took a taxi into central London. His hotel was near the Embankment and he checked in at 10pm. He wasn't hungry and after dropping his bag in the room he took the lift downstairs and went into the lounge bar. His mood had darkened during his flight and he moved away from the bar and chose a table in the corner. The large Spanish brandy might help him get some sleep but he was wired and could only think of the morning when he'd begin the hunt for his kilo of fentanyl. He'd trusted those in his organisation to deliver and he would find Frank. Swallowing the last of his drink he made his way back to his room.

**

The following morning Rico left the hotel at 5.30 and started walking. Twenty minutes later he flagged a black cab and gave him the name of the street in south east London where Frank lived.

'You're lucky mate. I'm just going home in that direction.'

It was light and the city was beginning to wake up when he told the driver to pull up at the top of Whitchurch Road. Stepping out he rang Frank's number but it went straight to message.

Walking up the right-hand side of the street he arrived at number 60. All the curtains were closed on both the ground floor and the top floor windows of the pre-war detached brick house. He rang the bell and waited, then rang it again. When he didn't get an answer, he walked round the side of the house and looked in through the French window at the rear of the building. It didn't appear as if anyone was around and Rico took a heavy knife from his pocket and jammed the blade into the crack between the door and the brick surround. He heard the click and simply slid the door open. No alarm.

He walked in and looked around. There was a sideboard to his right and he began pulling out the drawers. There was nothing of any consequence and he moved through to the kitchen. Opening the fridge, he checked the sell-by date on the milk and it was three days over. Nothing to tell him Frank had been around in the recent past. Going upstairs, he tossed all three bedrooms and after pulling out all the drawers, he ripped open the mattresses and found nothing of any interest. Going into the bathroom he pulled the side of the bath off and looked underneath then removed the top of the cistern and threw it into the floor. He plunged his hand in the water and found nothing.

Coming downstairs, he ripped the sitting room apart, checking under the carpet for any loose floorboards. There were none. Then he went into the kitchen and lit up the gas on each ring. Spraying some cooking oil over the window curtain he draped it near the gas rings. Leaving as he came in, he walked away and

91

didn't look back as he heard a loud bang in the distance behind him.

His frustration boiled up and he walked for two miles before hailing a taxi. As he sat in the back, he knew Frank had gone. He had been his Mr London, his Mr Fixit, the man who controlled all the distribution as the drugs arrived in the UK. He was trusted implicitly and had co-ordinated the removal of Susan Long. As the taxi moved slowly through heavy morning traffic, he knew the only thing that would bring information would be fear.

Back at his hotel he headed to his room and opened the mini bar. He swirled the brandy around in his glass before taking a sip. He had some work to do to find Frank and Salvador but he knew where to find the private detective. He had to be heavily involved and would have information. He downed his drink and went over to the mini bar for another.

Chapter Twenty-Three

Frank was holed up in a rented flat above a dry-cleaners in Finsbury Park. He was short of cash but he had a kilo of one of the most potent opioids known and he was due to meet with his first buyer in the morning. He'd masterminded the switch of tracker and cars as Salvador drove north but he knew Rico would be on his way to locate the missing consignment. His mobile was an untraceable pay-as-you-go and his contacts were written on a scrap of paper in a side pocket of his large sports bag. He'd left his house with enough clothes for two weeks and would plan his future when he'd sold on the drugs stash.

His belly was telling him to eat and he had seen a nice pub on the corner about three hundred yards away on the Seven Sisters Road. He pushed the pack of fentanyl into the space behind the bath panel in his tiny bathroom and checked his wallet. He had a hundred pounds in cash, which would see him through tonight.

As he pushed the door of the pub open he immediately felt at home. The aroma of food hit his nostrils and he selected a stool at the bar. The menu was limited but he chose roast chicken with French fries and ordered a beer. He'd taken his first sip when the dramatic film of a fire came up on the giant Sky News screen at the end of the bar. He whispered to himself, 'Oh, my God, that's my house.' As he watched the blue lights of the fire engines dancing in front of the huge red and orange glow of his home being destroyed, he knew his life was changed forever. His home would be gone in the sparks shooting up into the sky. Unable to watch anymore, he placed his pint on the bar and walked out to the street. He knew Rico had arrived.

Chapter Twenty-Four

Jack had left Eva's at eight in the morning after she'd insisted on making him a cooked breakfast. It had been an amazing night but he was aware he'd crossed the line by getting intimate with a client. It was the first time he'd done it, but as he walked back to the Tube station he decided fate had thrown them together. Everyone had a right to happiness and in Eva's case it had been impossible to resist. That's the way he was going to see it.

As the underground rattled and screeched its way towards central London, he thought of his options for progressing the case. The process didn't take long. He'd go straight to his office in Kensington and run some of his deep search data bases. He had the London phone number taken from Juan's desk pad to check and the Audi coming in through Dover. It was something.

He let himself into his office and listened to his phone messages. None were urgent and he switched the percolator on to make some coffee. Logging on to his computer he checked his emails and found two that looked promising as new business. He walked across to the coffee machine and poured himself a mug. There was no milk, so it was going to be black.

Back at his desk he keyed in a password and accessed his private database. He checked out the phone number he'd taken from Juan's garage and the address came up on the screen. It was in Whitchurch Road in Lewisham. Logging off from the private website, he Googled the address and began reading of a fire and explosion that had gutted a detached house in the road yesterday. The report said the house was owned by a Frank Portman who was not thought to have been in residence when the fire broke out and had not yet been contacted by police. The fire was being treated as suspicious and witnesses were being sought. Jack wrote down the name and visited other news sites to see if any new information was being reported. One gave an update of a man seen near the house around the time of the fire but no description had been given. Jack Googled the name Frank Portman but received no hits of any relevance. As he sipped his coffee he thought about what he had just learned. The fire was certainly too much of a coincidence and if deliberate, he suspected others connected with the case could be on the list for a visit.

His thoughts were disturbed by the mail delivery rattling through his letter box. He thumbed through it but it was all junk. As he went back to his desk it struck him that he no longer needed an office with all its upkeep. Everything of any importance arrived either on his computer or his mobile phone. He resolved to give notice and vacate it at the end of his lease. He'd miss the buzz of Kensington but not the commute from his apartment in Maida Vale.

He needed a break on this case and looked up the mobile number of his old friend Matt in the London Met.

'Hi, Matt, it's Jack Barclay. How's things?'

'Long time no hear, Jack. What's up?'

'I'm working on a case but have hit a wall at the moment. I have some information you may find interesting.'

Matt chuckled. 'I'm all ears. Maybe we can help each other.'

'I'm working for the sister of the woman who was killed when a guy fell out of the Majestic Hotel in west London.'

'I remember it,' Matt said. 'I'm not working the case but I know who is.'

'I've spent a bit of time in Malaga where she lived and dug up one or two things. You may know all this, but the dead woman was likely trafficking cocaine to the UK and her death is probably linked to the cartel she became involved with. I've got a name for you and I think he's at the top of the London end of the operation. Does Frank Portman mean anything to you?'

'Nope, but go on.'

'I think his house in Lewisham was burned to the ground yesterday. By all accounts he wasn't inside when it went up and he's gone to ground. I think another shipment of drugs came in by road through Dover from Malaga four days ago. The ferry was P&O and they were thought to be in a black Audi A6 with Spanish plates. That's all I know on that, but I'm sure there'll be some record of the registration.'

'I'll pass this all on, Jack. What are you looking for?'

'Frank Portman must have upset someone. He may be dead. The one thing that would help me is knowing if the shipment went to plan. I'm assuming Portman received the consignment but then something happened. Someone has the drugs and if it's Portman, the mob will be after him. If you hear of anything I'd be grateful for a call.'

'Leave it with me, Jack. Likewise let me know if you have any developments. We must meet up for a beer. I think it's your turn.'

Jack laughed. 'It probably is. I'll keep in touch. Speak soon.' He ended the call and sat back in his chair before putting his left leg on the desk. As he took a sip of his lukewarm coffee he thought of Eva and picked up his mobile.

'Hi, it's me. Can you talk?'

'Just a quickie. How are you?'

'I'm fine. At the office. Things have slowed down but the day's not over yet. Have you heard anything more about Susan?'

'Nope, not a thing. As far as I know, the toxicology reports aren't back. I'll just have to be patient.' Jack grunted and Eva asked, 'Will I see you tonight?'

'I hope so. Let's go out.'

'Hmm, I'm going to be working on for a bit to finish a report. How about just coming over and I'll rustle something up.'

'Sounds good. About eight.'

'That would be lovely. See you later, Jack.'

He made a mental note to buy some flowers.

***

Tony had been told to meet up with the driver of a black BMW 3 series and he pulled into the car park of the Crown ten minutes early. Choosing a spot at the back, he waited for his contact to arrive. He checked his wallet to make sure the cash was there and nervously thrummed his fingers on the steering wheel and kept looking at his watch. 'Come on.' He saw the time creep up to seven o'clock and his anxiety grew. He didn't know who he was meeting and it could be a set-up. At five minutes past seven he started his engine and put his car into gear. As he released the hand brake, a black BMW 3 Series turned into the car park and headed slowly in his direction. Tony kept his engine running and waited. The black car drove nose first alongside him and the driver's window was lowered. Tony did the same and saw a figure with a red baseball cap stuck well down on his forehead and a black zip-up jacket with a high collar that covered his lower face. All that was visible was a pointed nose.

'You got the money?'

'Yes, I have it. Have you got the stuff?'

'It's here and it's the best. Try it if you like.' Just as he said it, Frank's phone rang and Tony heard him lapse into Spanish. He heard the agitation in Frank's voice and was sure Malaga was mentioned.

Frank cut the call and turned back to Tony. 'You want to test it?'

Tony shook his head and said, 'I'll take your word for it. Here's the three hundred if you want to count it.'

The dealer stretched out his hand holding the cocaine and exchanged it for the envelope in Tony's hand. The man flicked through the notes inside and grunted as he stuffed the envelope inside his jacket. 'You've got my number if you need any more.'

Tony placed the packet of white powder in the glove compartment and waited for the car to leave the car park. Moving forward, he drove out to join the heavy Friday traffic and turned on the radio to Jazz FM. He smiled to himself as he thought of the weekend ahead.

Chapter Twenty-Five

Rebecca put a brush through her dark curly hair and chose a pair of mustard-coloured tasselled earrings by Jack & Freda. She looked in the full-length mirror and was pleased

with her choice of a high-necked white blouse above her favourite blue jeans. The excitement was building in her mind and it was only just past seven o'clock. The pizza she'd bought on the way home from work lay by the cooker, waiting to be oven baked. Popping open a bottle of Prosecco she poured herself a glass and walked through to her living room and pulled the curtains. After plumping up the cushions on the sofa she cleared the magazines off the glass-topped coffee table and stashed them underneath. Fetching a kitchen roll she wiped the table top to make sure it was clear of any debris. She spent the next fifteen minutes checking text messages on her phone and answering some from friends asking about tomorrow night's party. She told them, 'Get here for eight 'cos it's going to be the best yet.' When her best friend Andrea texted her she said, 'Get here for seven and we'll get a little bit of flying speed up. Lol!'

Tony arrived early and when she opened the door, gasped when she saw the bunch of red roses clutched in his hand.

'Hi, Bex.'

'Well, hi. They're gorgeous.' She stepped forward and kissed him. 'Come in.'

Rebecca put the flowers in some water and walked back into the living room with the Prosecco. As she placed the bottle on the coffee table, Tony reached into his pocket. The small bag looked like all the others they had seen since they began their habit.

'I'll just get the glasses, honey.'

Tony carefully opened the bag and emptied out the contents on the table and began shaping them out into lines with the edge of a credit card. Rebecca re-appeared with two glasses.

'We can eat later. I've bought pizza.'

Tony looked up from the table. 'Yeah, there's plenty of time for that. Let's have some fun and work up an appetite.'

Rebecca clinked glasses and said, 'Sounds good to me.' She took a large sip from her wine glass and sat down next to Tony. 'God, I've been waiting all week for this.'

Tony had rolled up a twenty-pound note and he handed it to her.

'Ladies first.'

Rebecca laughed and placed her glass on the table. Taking the rolled-up note from Tony, she bent down and pressed her finger onto her left nostril. Grinning at Tony she stuck the rolled note into her right nostril and began hoovering up the white powder.

***

Tony was waiting for Rebecca to pass him the rolled-up note when he heard her gasp, 'Oh, my God.'

Her body stiffened and within seconds she began to shake.

'Bex, what's happened?' He dropped his drink and lunged towards her to support her head. She began to gurgle, and panic gripped him as he saw her pupils begin to dilate and her lips turn a dark blue colour.

'Oh, Christ, Bex speak to me. Say something. Please God, no.'

He heard a rasping noise from her open mouth and she began to vomit. Sweat appeared on her forehead and her body began to jerk.

'Bex. Oh, God, Bex.'

She stopped shaking and went limp in his arms. As her mouth went slack, her body fell against his.

'Oh, Jesus, God. Becky, Becky my love, say something. Speak to me.'

Tears ran down his face and he screamed out her name as he began feverishly pumping her chest. He increased the pressure, but she wasn't responding. Wiping the vomit from her lips he stuck his fingers inside her mouth and tried to clear any obstruction in her throat. Kneeling on the floor he held her nostrils closed and placed his mouth on hers. As his tears mixed with the mucus on her purple-coloured face he frantically blew into her mouth. There was no sign of movement but her eyes with their now pin-point pupils remained open. He looked down on her lifeless body and sobbed uncontrollably. He knew he'd killed the woman he loved. Searching for his phone he punched 999 as Rebecca watched him with unseeing eyes.

Chapter Twenty-Six

Rico took a taxi to Kensington. The Tube system baffled him and he didn't like being underground. The High Street was busy with shoppers seeking out the high-end boutiques and he listened to the many foreign languages as he made his way to Jack Barclay's office. He needn't have been concerned about being recognised or spotted as everyone seemed to be looking at their mobile phones.

A pale September light shone through the light cloud as he checked the door numbers. He came to the one he was looking for, but kept walking. Crossing the road, he stood and looked over at Barclay's office. It was an elegant Victorian six-storey building with an arched doorway. He watched as a well-dressed woman approached and pressed one of the buttons on the right-hand side. The door opened after a few seconds and she disappeared inside. He waited a little longer and crossed to the building. Looking down the small cards below each button he spotted 'Jack Barclay. Private Investigator'.

Rico pressed the buzzer and waited before hearing, 'Can I help you?'

'Hello, Mr Barclay. You come recommended and I need some help. Could I come up and see you?'

Jack looked at the image on the entry phone screen and saw a 40ish man with an aquiline nose, thin lips and a dark complexion. His right eye brow was scarred.

Jack lied, 'I don't meet people without an appointment in my office but there's a coffee shop across the road. It's called Bean Me Up. Can you see it?'

'Yeah, I see it.'

'I'll meet you there in ten minutes. I'm just finishing something here.' Jack switched his mobile phone to camera and captured a shot of the face in the entry phone screen.

The man replied, 'Whatever.'

The face disappeared from the screen and Jack moved across to the window and looked down to the street below. He watched as the figure retreated from the doorway and began walking down the busy pavement. He kept watching but there was no sign of him making his way across the street to the café. It looked to Jack as if his visitor didn't want a meeting in public. He grabbed his keys before locking the office and sprinting down the stairs.

He turned left and made his way quickly along the pavement, hugging the buildings as his eyes swept the pedestrians ahead of him. He saw his target after a couple of minutes waiting for a green light at a crossing about fifty yards ahead. Jack hung back and watched the man cross the road and hold up his arm as a taxi approached. The black cab stopped and Rico climbed in. The taxi did a U-turn and headed back towards central London. There was no other cab in sight and Jack made his way back to the office, feeling sure his visitor would find him again.

***

Two paramedics arrived at Rebecca's flat in sixteen minutes to find a girl being given CPR by a hysterical young man. Going by the purple colour of her face and the powder on the glass-topped table, they knew the answer before asking the question.

The young paramedic knelt by Rebecca and looked up at Tony. 'How long ago?'

He whispered, 'About twenty minutes.'

'Did you take any?'

'No, I let Rebecca go first.' His voice broke as he said, 'I wish it had been me.'

The medic was feeling for a pulse on Rebecca's neck and the other placed an oxygen mask over her mouth and nose before shining a small torch into her eyes.

The older medic looked at Tony and asked, 'What has she taken? I'm Kevin by the way.' Then he nodded at his partner. 'This is James.'

'It was cocaine. Or at least it was supposed to be.'

Kevin looked across at his medic partner who shook his head. Rebecca remained lifeless and Tony began shouting her name. Kevin looked for any sign of movement from the still form at his side. James began slapping her face gently and called her name close to her ear.

There was a knock at the door and two uniformed police officers came in just as Tony was making his way across the living room.

The officers took in the scene and remained silent as the medics worked to try and revive Rebecca. Kevin had started CPR and kept going for what seemed like an age to Tony. He stopped after five minutes and felt for a pulse. Lifting the oxygen mask, he put an ear to her mouth and nose. He looked up at Tony. 'I'm sorry.'

The police officers glanced at the medics as Tony began to scream Rebecca's name. Everyone heard a loud wailing sound that built up to a crescendo of noise and Tony sank to his knees sobbing uncontrollably. One of the police officers turned away and spoke quietly into his radio.

Chapter Twenty-Seven

Jack ducked into a coffee shop, ordered a cappuccino and chose a table by the window. Bringing out his phone, he scrolled down to the image he'd captured on the entry phone. As he looked at the pock-marked face, he took in the coldness of the man's eyes. A man with violence embedded in his soul. If he had one.

Uploading the image, he tapped out a message under it. 'I think this guy could be of interest to me and maybe to you, too. Call if you'd like to talk.' He sent it to Matt at his private email address. A waiter brought his coffee and his phone rang as he was about to take his first sip.

'Jack, it's Matt. Nice-looking guy. I'm sending it on and I should know pretty soon if we have anything on him. What's your interest?'

Jack turned towards the window and kept his voice low. 'It's only a hunch but I think he could be connected to Susan Long. He turned up unannounced at my office and tried to blag his way in.'

'Could be interesting. I'll get back to you.'

The pavements were busy with lunchtime crowds and the walk back to his office was slow. When Jack pushed the door into his office, his mobile rang and he took the call from Matt.

'I think your hunch was right. His image is known to Interpol and I'm waiting for a more detailed report. He lives in Spain.'

Jack sat down in his chair and said, 'Will you be able to give me any more when you get the report?'

'I think we can exchange information to progress our enquiry. I'll put you down as an informant.'

Jack laughed and replied, 'Don't forget my fee.'

After the call ended Jack rang Eva. She was on message. 'Hi I'm busy right now but I'll call you when I can.'

Jack ended the call and thought about the conversation he'd just had with Matt. If the man was connected to Susan, how did he know about him? As he pondered his own question his phone rang.

'Hi, handsome.'

'Hi, Eva. How's things?'

'Busy, but in a good way. You called, sir.'

'I was just checking in. I think I'm making some progress but I'll tell you later. How about your favourite Italian tonight?'

'That would be lovely. I could be ready for eight.'

'Eight it is. I'll book Luigi's and pick you up at quarter to.'

'See you then. Don't be late.'

101

He wondered how much he should say about the day's events. He knew he and Eva had left a trail in Malaga and they were now at a disadvantage and probably in danger.

***

They arrived at Luigi's by taxi and were shown to a table at the side of the restaurant. Jack chose a bottle of red and they ordered from the à la carte menu. Touching glasses as they waited for their starters to arrive Eva asked, 'So, how's it going?'

Jack hesitated and replied, I think I've made some progress but it's still early days. I've a lead on someone who I think is connected to all this. I'll know more in the next few days.'

A thoughtful look crossed Eva's face.

'What's up?'

'How many dead people have you seen, Jack?'

He was surprised at the sudden change in the mood and said, 'When I was in the police force, I saw my fair share but that was a few years ago. Nowadays I don't see many, in fact I can't remember when I last saw one. Why do you ask?'

Eva looked down before replying. 'We lost our parents years ago but Susan and I were too young to see them at the funeral home. They both died of cancer within a short time of one another and we were told we should remember them when they were healthy. When I had to identify Susan it was such a shock and I'm having nightmares now. It seems to be some sort of delayed reaction, but I think I need some help to come to terms with what has happened.'

Jack took hold of her hand and said, 'It's been a shocking experience and it may only be kicking in now. You must let me know how I can help you.'

'Thank you. I just need to talk it out. The Malaga trip filled my days and didn't give me too much thinking time but I have a feeling of dread now.'

The waiter arrived with their food and Eva leaned back as he set the plate in front of her.

'I'm okay, Jack, just a bit down right now.'

As they ate, he was relieved he hadn't gone into detail about the day's events. They moved away from talking about Susan, and Jack suggested they think about a holiday together in Scotland. By the time coffee arrived they were both convinced a bit of time north of the border would be just what they needed to get them out of big city life for a week. As they sipped their coffee, Jack's phone bleeped with a text. 'Until next time.'

As he placed his phone back in his pocket, Eva looked at him quizzically. 'Business?'

'Yeah, just routine stuff.'

As Jack signalled for the bill, Eva said, 'How about my place for a nightcap. Maybe a Scotch?'

Jack smiled and nodded as the waiter arrived with the bill.

***

They reached Eva's flat and Jack said, 'Let's save the nightcap.' They went straight to bed and made love.

Much later, he caught the Tube back to central London. He felt happy as he thought of Eva and he idly picked up a crumpled copy of the London Evening Standard as he sat down in the carriage. A report on page three told of the death of a young woman in Shoreditch. Her boyfriend was being questioned in connection with her death although no charges had been made. The cause of death was thought to have been a drug overdose.

Jack let himself into his flat and checked his landline for messages. He thought about the drug story in the newspaper and tried to make connections before climbing into bed.

***

The phone woke him in the morning and glancing bleary-eyed at the clock, he realised it was only 7.00am.

'Matt, it's early and you've caught me without any clothes.'

'Far too much information, but anyway, I've got some news for you if you have a minute?'

'Of course.'

'Have you heard of the drug death of a young woman in Shoreditch two nights ago?'

'Yes, I read about it.'

'Off the record, there may be a connection to the Susan Long case.'

'Oh, yes?'

'The boyfriend is beside himself. Thinks he is totally responsible for her death. Well, he probably is, but as far as we can tell at the moment, he was sold some adulterated cocaine. The tests are not finished, but going by the speed of death and symptoms it could be there was fentanyl heavily cut into it.'

'How come her boyfriend survived?'

'She went first and he was about to run a line when she began fitting and choking.'

Jack let his breath out. 'Poor woman. Jesus, you never know what you're buying nowadays.'

'Thing is, Jack, and this could just be a coincidence, there may be a Spanish connection to the source of the cocaine.'

'How so?'

'The boyfriend's name is Tony. He's well educated and in his late twenties and a weekend user. He said the stuff came from a new supplier who was recommended to him by his old one. They met in a pub car park and the dealer's phone rang as they were doing the deal. At one time the conversation lapsed into Spanish. The seller called himself Chris and although he was trying to keep his voice down, Tony heard Malaga mentioned. His Spanish is average but he said his dealer was nervous, almost scared of something. We're chasing down a few leads and checking CCTV at the pub but there may have been false plates on the car. It's only my theory but your visitor to the office yesterday could very well be connected. I reckon it's a consignment gone missing and if it's fentanyl then watch out, Jack. This stuff is cut into shit cocaine to give it a boost and its street value is mind blowing. I'll keep in touch. The boyfriend is in shock and needs a few days, but let me know if your visitor turns up again. Even you might need some help.'

'Thanks, Matt. Appreciated and I'll keep in touch.'

He ended the call and thought about the conversation he'd just had. Most of all, he wondered what on earth Susan had got herself into and who she met with on her visits to London.

***

Rico had moved out of the hotel on the Embankment after arguing with the night manager over a room service charge and he had found a small hotel in Victoria near the coach station. The area was packed with tourists from all parts of the world and he blended in quite easily. His hotel booking was under an assumed name and he'd paid cash without being asked for ID. Breakfasts were simple affairs and not dissimilar to those in small European hotels.

Pulling out the chair at a small table at the back of the breakfast room he saw a copy of the previous night's London Evening Standard. He sipped his coffee and cut open his croissant before idly glancing at yesterday's news. He stopped eating as he came to the story of the drug death in Shoreditch. The description of the scene lacked detail but Rico knew only fentanyl killed an adult that quickly. He read the report twice before tearing the page out and stuffing it into his inside pocket. He had two names now. One was alive and one was dead.

Back in his poky room he went onto Facebook and typed in Rebecca's name. She had chosen not to divulge any personal information about herself but anyway she was dead. Then he searched Tony Northwood. There was some personal information and Rico wrote on a scrap of paper that he worked at Screech Marketing in London. He Googled the company and wrote down their address and telephone number. Fishing the newspaper cutting from his pocket he re-read it and noted the drugs were purchased the day before the death of the woman. He would find out where the exchange took place and anyone who had seen anything. Unzipping his carry-on case, he brought out an unregistered pay-as-you-go phone and rang Screech Marketing.

'Hello, you don't know me but I'm Tony Northwood's uncle. I'm calling from Spain and we've just heard the terrible news about Rebecca. My wife and I would like to send our condolences but we know he has moved address recently. I wonder if you would be so kind as to let us have his new one?'

The female voice said, 'It's so awful. We are all in shock here but I'm not supposed to give out any personal information about employees.'

Rico replied, 'I know, I'm in business myself and I quite understand, but maybe just this once you would help because of the tragedy. We would like to support Tony.'

The girl's voice said, 'Just give me a moment please.'

A few moments later she was back on the line and read out his address.

'Thank you so much and please accept our sincere condolences and prayers.' He clicked off the call, noted down the address and let his breath out. A step nearer locating Frank.

***

Jack quickly found all the information on Tony Northwood from one of his data bases. He knew the guy would be in bits over the death of his girlfriend because no matter how people tried to console him, he was the one who had bought the cocaine. He Googled fentanyl and read up on its effects. As he read, he began to understand the carnage this opioid had wreaked around the world. It was added to cocaine as the purity dropped along the supply chain. With it being fifty times more potent than heroin, a few grains of it could kill an adult. As he read on he realised it was being added in such a random way to low-grade cocaine as to render much of it lethal. Rebecca must have snorted the line that contained most of the added fentanyl. Jack winced as he read that the underlying cause of death is suffocation. He now fully realised the implication of Matt's warning to him. If a huge consignment of fentanyl had been stolen, the street value could be in the hundreds of thousands, not to mention the death rate. He thought of Rebecca and her last petrified moments.

***

Next morning Jack sat in his kitchen chair and learned the results of the coroner's report on the death of Susan Long and the man who fell from the hotel window. The faller was from Estonia and named Niculas Kaasik. He'd been living in a hostel in Tooting. His sole income seemed to be from begging around the theatre queues in the West End and the post mortem showed high levels of cocaine and heavy alcohol use. It had also been established that he was dead when he fell.

Susan Long's neck had been broken with the impact and she'd also sustained fractures to her upper body. Death had been instantaneous.

As he read the report, Jack took a small amount of comfort from the fact that Eva's sister had not suffered and the man who was hurled out of the hotel window certainly didn't know his part in the murder of a woman driving through London.

It made for grim reading and had all the trademarks of organised crime. The logistics of getting a drug-fuelled man into the hotel, dead or alive, needed a lot of luck or inside help. Re-filling his coffee mug, he moved through to his living room and balanced the mug on the side of the armchair. He wondered about the method used to kill Susan. It could so easily have gone wrong and there had to be a reason for the risk. As he sipped his drink he could only think it was an attempt to make it look like an accident. He jotted down some notes from the medical report before calling Eva. He needed to see her and talk about her sister's death. He left a message on her phone.

***

Frank had read about Rebecca's death and immediately connected it to his fentanyl sale to the guy in the pub car park. He didn't like it. Not because of the girl's death, but the publicity it would create. He needed to get rid of the stuff as quickly as possible and he began making some phone calls. He put the word out that he was looking for a wholesale buyer. Someone with enough cash to buy close on a kilo of fentanyl. He knew exactly what he'd do when he landed a buyer. He would be out of London the same day and out of the drug business. There was a small house he knew was available in a small village in south west France near the Spanish border. His new name and passport could be ready as soon as he had the money to pay for them and he would disappear forever.

An hour later his phone rang, and a male voice asked for him by name.

'Who's calling?'

'It's Charlie. You don't know me, but you have been recommended to me.'

'Oh, yeah?'

'I need some stuff. Quite a lot actually.'

'What sort of stuff?'

'You know. Charlie.' There was a chuckle at the other end.

'Even if I could help, I don't know who you are.'

'I supply free parties in the country outside London. Big ones and I've got one coming up in Oxfordshire next week. I need the best and money isn't a problem. Most of the kids are loaded. I can meet you in the open anywhere you choose and I guarantee I'll be on my own. I need three hundred and fifty grams and the purity needs to be at least seventy per cent.'

Frank stayed silent for a few seconds then said. 'Must be a big party. I can do that. Give me a couple of days.'

Charlie replied, 'No problem. The party is not until next weekend. What's your price?'

'It'll be £80 a bag.'

'Make it £70 and you've got a deal.'

Frank replied, '£75.'

'Okay. That's top rate but it better be top quality too. I'll have cash in fifties and twenties and you can name the meet-up place on the day. At that price I need it in bags.'

Frank had done the sums and the deal would net him around twenty grand. This would get him away to his place in France.

'Give me your number and I'll get back to you when I have the stuff ready. Just make sure you're on your own when we meet.'

'Don't worry, I will be. I've got a business to look after as well.'

Frank just grunted and wrote down Charlie's number. As soon as he ended the call he began ringing round his contacts. He needed some credit fast and a lot of low-grade cocaine. In just over half an hour he'd spoken to six dealers and organised deliveries with the promise he'd introduce them to Charlie. The price varied but he knew the quality would also vary between 20% and shit. He smiled to himself and knew that with some fentanyl cut into it, some rich kids were going to have the time of their lives.

Chapter Twenty-Eight

Jack waited until the evening to call Tony Northwood's mobile. It was picked up quickly.

'Tony, you don't know me. My name is Jack Barclay and I'm a private investigator. I believe I can identify the dealer who sold you the drugs that killed Rebecca. I am so sorry for the loss you have suffered.'

'How did you find this number?'

'It's not very difficult these days.'

'Look, the police are dealing with everything and anyway I don't even know who you are.'

Jack chose his words carefully. 'You are in danger because you have met the dealer. He is being hunted by the mob who probably owned the cocaine sold to you. You are the link and if I can find you then so can they.'

'So, what's in it for you to help me?'

'Like you, I am working to find justice. My client lost her sister to this outfit. It's personal for me and there's no charge to you.'

Jack heard a grunt and Tony said, 'I'll think about it. My head isn't in too good a place right now.'

'I can understand that and I'm sorry for ringing you so soon but please don't wait too long. As the police investigation builds up, those responsible could leave the country at any time.'

'Okay. I've got your number now. What did you say your name was?'

'It's Jack Barclay and please call me soon.' The line went dead and Jack ran his hand through his grey-flecked black hair. He decided to ring Tony back if he didn't hear from him in twenty-four hours. He called Eva and left a message asking her to call him. His mobile rang almost immediately and Jack heard the voice of his solicitor, Angela Stevens.

'Hi, Angela. What's new?'

'Hi, Jack. I've completed all the papers for the ending of your lease for the Kensington office. You'll be a free man in twelve weeks. If the landlord finds a new tenant inside that time frame then it could be sooner.'

'Thanks, Angela. I'll miss that part of London but not the rent. Just send the papers and I'll sign them and get them back to you.'

'Will do.'

Chapter Twenty-Nine

The dark blue cap Rico bought from the market stall bore no markings, but it looked sort of official from a distance. As he made his way to Tony's apartment block he stopped at a florist and bought an expensive bouquet of flowers.

The girl serving him said, 'She's a lucky girl.'

He just smiled.

Parking in a street a short distance away, he pulled the cap well down on his forehead. When he reached the door, he held the bouquet up and made sure the cap was visible. Ringing the bell, Rico heard footsteps and a voice shouted, 'Who is it?'

'Fun Flowers, sir.'

Tony had opened the door a few inches, looked at him and asked, 'Who are you from?'

Just as he finished his question, Rico kicked the door open, slamming it against Tony's legs and Rico launched himself forward. The sudden force knocked Tony off balance and he staggered against the side wall.

Rico turned towards him and saw Tony use the wall as purchase to throw himself forward. The two fell to the floor wrestling amongst the pile of crushed flowers. Rico felt a punch to the side of his face and tried to bring his knee round to land a blow to Tony's body. As Rico tasted blood from his lip he knew he'd underestimated the strength of his opponent. He managed to land a blow with his fist but it didn't have the power to hurt and as he took another heavy punch on the chin, he felt his strength weakening.

Tony was shouting out now and with the door wide open, Rico knew it was only a matter of time before someone came to find out what the commotion was. He leapt up and disappeared out into the corridor and left Tony staggering to his feet.

As neighbours' doors opened, all that could be heard was the angry shouting from a man walking quickly towards the main entrance of the apartment block.

***

From the description Tony was giving over the phone, Jack realised the attacker was the man who had called unannounced at his office.

'He seems to be desperate for information and he's likely to come after you again. Is there anywhere you can go for a few days?'

'I can go and stay with my parents for a while. Do you really think he'll come back?'

'Anything could happen. It looks as if you are his only known link to the guy who sold you the cocaine. If it was cocaine.'

Tony paused and asked, 'Do you know the name of the guy who attacked me? How did he know where I lived?' Tony's questions were tumbling out as the adrenalin continued to course through him.

'I have a name but it is almost bound to be false and finding someone's address is not difficult nowadays.'

'But why is he after me? Rebecca is gone. What does he want from me?'

'He knows you met the dealer and he wants to find him. Something has gone badly wrong inside their organisation and you've been caught up in it. Have the police taken a statement from you?'

'Yes and they were also checking for CCTV at the main entrance but I don't think it works.'

Jack repeated his request that Tony should move out for a few days. 'Can you have some time off?'

'Yes, my boss has been very understanding. I can't face anyone at the moment. I just think of Rebecca all the time and I feel so low.' Tony's voice broke as he spoke.

'Have some time with your parents, Tony and I'll keep in touch with you. Let the police know where you are. I'm sure they will be staying close.'

Jack barely heard the thank you as the line went dead.

***

The post mortem had confirmed the presence of fentanyl in the cocaine inhaled by Rebecca and she had died quickly of suffocation. Jack knew the service would be harrowing but he also knew there was a chance of Rico turning up.

The church had been full to overflowing and it was obvious how much Rebecca had been loved by so many people. At the end of the service he joined the congregation and filed out amidst the sobbing of relatives and friends.

Black clouds had gathered to the west as everyone made their way out of the church for the burial. He had parked his car nearby and he hung back, standing under a large oak tree two hundred yards from the grave site.

Jack watched closely as people congregated. Tony was with Rebecca's family, but he was walking behind them with his head down. Jack began to think he had anticipated too much when he caught sight of a man who looked oddly dressed for a funeral. He was wearing a heavy dark-brown coat and a wide-brimmed hat pulled down over his brow. He appeared at the back of the mourners and was looking around the gathering. Although he was over one hundred and fifty yards away, Jack knew it was him. The figure remained at a distance from the graveside and no one seemed to take any notice of him.

When the graveside ceremony drew to a close, Jack watched as the man moved in behind the mourners as they began to make their way back towards the parked cars. He saw Tony speaking briefly with Rebecca's parents. Everyone seemed to be in tears and the conversations were short. The man in the hat moved closer to them and as Tony walked away the stranger changed direction and followed him. Jack began walking towards them as the stranger put his hand in his right coat pocket to pull out what appeared to be a knife.

'Tony!' Jack's shout echoed round the cemetery and he immediately shouted again, 'Tony, look out!'

Tony and the man with the knife both spun round and Jack sprinted towards them. He shouted, 'No' as much as to alert everyone to the danger, as warning Tony. He dodged round two tall grave stones and dived towards the knifeman just as he was about to reach Tony. The body charge knocked the knifeman off balance and Jack caught him full in the jaw with his right fist. The knife was still in the assailant's hand and Jack shouted to Tony to stay back. The knifeman shouted 'Cabron' as he retreated and began slashing the air with the knife.

Jack placed himself in front of Tony and as other mourners began arriving, the man in the hat dived into their midst. Jack ran after him and spotted a hat in the small crowd. He made his way towards it and found an elderly man paying his respects to one of the family. After searching around the immediate area and looking at cars moving out towards the main gate he knew he'd lost him. Returning to Tony he checked he was okay and took him to one side.

'Did you recognise him?'

'Yeah, it was the guy who delivered the flowers.'

'Are you sure?'

'It was him alright. Thanks for the warning.'

They both heard the sirens and knew there was some lengthy questioning ahead. Tony covered his face with the palms of his hands and exhaled loudly.

Jack touched his shoulder. 'We'll find him.'

Chapter Thirty

Frank needed the cocaine to look and test top grade. Well, at least the bags that Charlie would sample. It was going to be a risk, but Frank knew how to keep the odds in his favour. The hundred and fifty grams of cocaine he was using off the street was 20% pure at best and he added benzocaine and crushed paracetamol into the mixing bowl. To bulk it further he added a good quantity of sodium bicarbonate and some powdered sugar. Donning a face mask, he opened the fentanyl and poured in around fifty grams. When he'd mixed it, he emptied all the powder into a large see-through plastic bag and laid it onto his scales. The bag weighed just over three hundred and ten grams and he tipped another thirty grams of fentanyl into the bag. He was short of the agreed amount and the last ten grams needed to be high grade cocaine for Charlie to select and test. He went to his suitcase and brought out a bag of almost pure cocaine and filled ten slightly oversized bags with the powder. Setting them aside he began the tedious process of filling over three hundred bags with a gram from the bag of mashed cocaine. After two hours, he lined the bags up in an empty cardboard box, placing the slightly oversized bags strategically along the row of mashed-up bags. After he'd finished, he stood back and inspected his handiwork. Running his fingers along the lines of bags, his finger always found the larger slightly raised ones. Satisfied he'd covered everything, he checked his watch and realised it was too late to go round to the local pub. Instead he went to his wardrobe and brought out a bottle of Scotch. Pouring himself an extra-large measure he sat down and switched on the television. He felt good and smiled to himself as he realised he'd have all the money he needed in forty-eight hours. He'd pack his things tomorrow and be ready for a quick exit the next day.

Chapter Thirty-One

Charlie had been on his phone for most of the day and things were going well with distributors piling in. The party was going to take place near Burford and the numbers were expected to be in the region of five hundred. Maybe more. He had made contact with known sellers and fixed a price. It was going to be a good night. He rang Frank.

'It's Charlie. Is everything ready?'

'Yeah, I'm all set. Everything you asked for and top grade.'

'Okay, good, just name your meeting place and I'll be there.'

'You have the cash?'

'Of course. Just as we agreed.'

'Fine. We'll meet tonight about seven. It'll be in London and I'll call you at four o'clock with the meeting place.'

'I look forward to it and by the way, I'll have scales and testing equipment with me.'

Frank said, 'I'd expect no less. See you at seven.'

Charlie heard the call being ended and sat back on his kitchen high stool. He was irritated that he didn't know the meeting place but at least he knew he wouldn't have to travel too far from his London pied-à-terre to do the deal. He made some more calls to Oxfordshire and agreed meeting times with sellers. Opening his rucksack, he took a last look at the money. It was all made up of used fifties and twenties and each wad had one thousand pounds tied with a rubber band. He smiled as he closed it.

Chapter Thirty-Two

Jack was running two other investigations alongside Eva's. His outgoings would soon be significantly reduced when he gave up his office in Kensington but his mortgage on the apartment in Maida Vale would keep him working for a long time to come. One of the cases he was working on involved a middle-aged man who was claiming disability benefit but was rumoured to be indulging in his passion for windsurfing off Bournemouth beach. He rang Eva.

'How do you fancy a weekend in Bournemouth?'

'I'd love that. Always great to get out of London for a bit. When can we go?'

'How about tomorrow night? I'll book a hotel with a sea view. I'll be working but only for part of the time.'

'That's fine with me. I'm excited, Jack. Can't wait, in fact.' She laughed and said, 'I've got to be in a meeting now but I'll call you later. I hope your seaside trip isn't too dangerous.'

'No, just a few photos and some phone video. With a bit of luck it shouldn't take long then we can relax and have fish and chips.'

'I like fish and chips but I don't need to go all the way to Bournemouth for them.'

Jack laughed and said, 'They'll be posh ones.'

'Oh, that's okay then. Why are we going, by the way?'

'I need to get some shots of a guy windsurfing who's supposed to be disabled.'

'But how do you know he'll be there?'

'Well, I can't be a hundred percent sure but the forecast is for full sunshine all weekend.'

'Shall I pack my swimsuit?'

'Why not. I'll pack mine.'

'Gotta go, Jack. Speak later.'

***

Jack's SAAB needed a good run after months of stop, start journeys in London and after picking up Eva they headed round the M25 to pick up the M3 for the south coast. It was 10am and the temperature was already nudging 22C. Eva was dressed in blue jeans and a black T-shirt.

'You look wonderful.' Jack had paid her the compliment when he first saw her that morning and he noticed the lightness in her step as she made her way to his car.

There were no holdups on the way and they pulled into Bournemouth just after midday.

'We can't book into the hotel until three o'clock so let's head for the beach.'

Eva suggested a light lunch and Jack nodded in agreement.

'You may spot your windsurfing man.'

'If we do then I can get some pictures, then work is finished and it'll be all pleasure.'

'I like the sound of that. All work and no play makes Jack a dull boy.'

Jack laughed and headed towards the beach. His information pointed to his man being near Boscombe pier and that he usually parked his distinctive metallic dark blue Ford van on the promenade. He'd seen a photograph of it and if it was here today, Jack felt sure he'd spot it. He'd shown the photo to Eva and as they neared the pier she shouted, 'There it is.'

Jack drove by slowly and there it was parked near an ice-cream parlour. He had to drive quite a distance before he found a parking space and after buying a three-hour ticket he checked that his phone was fully charged. Turning round in his seat, Jack stretched his arm round behind and picked up his Cannon SLR.

'Right, let's go and take some pictures. We're a couple of tourists out for a romantic stroll in the sunshine.'

'I think I can manage that.' Eva stepped out of the car to wait for Jack to come around and join her. She linked arms with him and they set off back towards the pier. As they approached it Jack said, 'There he is.' He pointed to a man in a blue and red wetsuit skimming along the outer surf towards the pier. He was about 500 yards off shore and Jack brought out a pair of compact binoculars from his pocket. As he focused on the surfer he knew from the description and photograph given that this was his man. He brought the camera up and zoomed into his target. Running the video, he caught him manoeuvring his board against the waves as if it was an extension of himself. He waited for almost an hour until he came ashore and he filmed him bringing all his kit on to the beach.

'Right, that's good. We can go now.' Jack kissed Eva and said, 'Let's get some lunch.' They found a small restaurant just behind the front and spent an hour over a small seafood platter for two and a glass of white wine each.

'This is so lovely, Eva. I hadn't realised how much I needed to be away from the city. To be with you just makes it complete.'

'Do you think our room will be ready?' Eva replied.

***

Frank placed the closed box with the cocaine into the boot of his BMW. Soon there would be no more lowlifes to contend with. He was about to retire to the South of France and enjoy the sunshine with maybe just a little bit of dealing here and there to keep the wolf from the door. He smiled as he got into the driver's seat and turned the ignition key, letting the engine idle. Picking up his mobile he rang Charlie.

'I've got your stuff. Have you got the money?'

'Yeah, I have it all exactly as you asked.'

'How well do you know the North Circular?'

'I use it from time to time.'

'There's a closed-down carpet warehouse just north of Hanger Lane on the left. You can't miss it. Painted orange and sale banners hanging from the front of the building. Go round the side and make sure you're on your own.'

'I'll be on my own, don't worry. What will you be driving?'

'I'll be in a black BMW 5. What will you be in?'

Charlie replied, 'A dark blue Mercedes M Class.'

'Okay, I'll see you then.'

***

Frank's drive to their rendezvous was slow even by London's standards but he drove round the deserted carpet warehouse car park to make sure he was on his own. As he waited for Charlie he checked out the building for CCTV but couldn't see any. Some windows had already been broken and graffiti had been sprayed on walls. He chose a spot where he could see the entrance from the North Circular and waited. As the meeting time approached he got out and retrieved the cocaine from the boot.

He saw the Mercedes pull in just after seven and drive slowly over to him. As he watched, the M Class reversed in next to him. They both lowered their windows simultaneously and eyeballed one another before nodding. Charlie reached across to the passenger seat and held up what looked like a black brief case and a smaller green plastic box. Calling over, he said to Frank, 'Your vehicle or mine?'

Frank waved him over to his car and Charlie climbed out and locked the doors. He waited until they were both in the BMW.

'I've got your money and a kit to test the purity.'

'That's fine.' Frank twisted round and brought the box from the back seat. 'It's all here and bagged up. Pick any one at random.'

Charlie ran his hand along the tightly-packed contents and stopped when his fingers felt the top of a bag. Tugging it out, he laid it on his lap and brought out his kit. Inside was a small sealed test tube with clear liquid at the bottom. Opening the bag, he tipped in a small amount of the white powder and gave the tube a shake. In a few seconds the liquid inside turned dark red and he re-sealed the bag. Running his hand across another row of bags, he pulled out another and repeated the test. Red again.

Frank said, 'Test as many as you like. You'll get the same result every time.'

'I'm happy with it. Do you want to check the money?' He handed Frank the rucksack and opened it for him. 'Count it.'

Frank brought out a wad of notes held together with a rubber band and began flicking through them. This batch consisted of fifty-pound notes and contained one thousand pounds. He selected another thicker wad and saw twenties as well as fifties. He counted them quickly and knew the total was another thousand pounds. He counted a total of twenty-six bundles and was happy he had his £26K. Turning to Charlie he asked, 'You happy?'

'Yeah, I'm good. Now let's get out of here.'

Frank assumed the rucksack was his and shut it before saying, 'Nice doing business with you.' Opening the door of the BMW, Charlie didn't look back. Both vehicles drove slowly out of the car park and turned in opposite directions after they exited.

***

Jack sat at his desk in his office and
wrote up his report on the benefit fraud windsurfer. Attaching the photos and video, he was satisfied he'd provided sufficient evidence for his client. He pressed 'send' and his thoughts drifted to the weekend he'd spent in Bournemouth. It had been idyllic and he had never felt such peace and happiness for a long time. He missed Eva when he wasn't with her and he began to think of a life away from being a private investigator. An old friend was due to arrive at lunchtime with his van, and Jack set about separating stuff to keep, from things to dump. He was grateful that his landlord had found a new tenant quickly.

As he came across forgotten case files and notes he began re-living some of the dangerous situations he'd found himself in over the years. He picked up a file and he'd written the name 'Finding Daniel' on the front. It took him back to the time when he had been asked to locate a child who had been abducted and taken abroad by the father. As he read the case he remembered how close he had come to being attacked by a guard dog when he eventually found the child on a farm in a remote part of France. Only a quick sprint and a passing motorist saved him from a mauling. The father hadn't known of Jack's presence and he was able to give the location of Daniel to his client. He heard later that the boy had been re-united with his mother in England.

With an hour to go before his friend arrived, he tried to speed up his packing and placed more items in the 'to keep' box than he'd intended. He made a last coffee and filled his favourite mug before sitting down on one of the boxes to wait.

His phone rang a few minutes later and the text read, 'Five minutes away.' He stood up and sighed as he drained the last of the coffee. Glancing at all the boxes to keep, he knew he'd have to look at a more serious de-clutter if he was to find space to work from his Maida Vale apartment. He walked out into the corridor and made his way to the front door.

***

Frank felt elated as he drove away from his meeting with Charlie. As he entered central London he began making calls to prepare for his quick exit. His first call was to a mate he knew from his local pub to offer him his BMW at well below its current value.

'What's wrong with it?'

Frank joined in the laughter and said, 'Not a thing but I need some cash on the hurry up to pay a debt.'

'Okay, I'm in the pub tonight and I'll have a look at it. I'll be there at nine.'

'Good. I'll see you then.'

When he got back to his room, he began packing his few belongings into a rucksack, stuffing the money near the bottom. The few things he didn't need went into a black plastic bag and he'd throw it in with the rubbish around the back of the take-away restaurants down the road. After checking his phone, he thought about the next forty-eight hours of his life. He'd be on Eurostar and across to France in no time. From Paris he'd take a coach to the South of France, give himself a new name and rent a mobile home on the coast for cash. He smiled as he opened a can of beer and sat down to wait until it was time to go to the pub and sell the car.

***

Rico was getting more pissed off by the minute. He'd made so many phone calls but couldn't get a lead on Frank's whereabouts. His pay-as-you-go phone had no contacts in the memory and he was relying on notes he'd made over the years of dealing drugs into the UK. As he lobbed his phone onto the table in front of him it rang out.

'Is that Rico?'

'Who's asking?'

'You just called a friend of mine. I believe you're looking for Frank?'

'I could be. Who's calling?'

'Call me Don.'

'Okay, what are you looking for?'

'I'll tell you where he is but I want a grand.'

'Why are you doing this?'

'Frank doesn't pay his debts so fuck him. I need some money.'

'How are you going to work it?'

'I'll be waiting for you near his place.'

'Okay. Where is he?'

'He's in a rented room in Finsbury Park. It's just off Seven Sisters Road.'

Rico said, 'You'd better be right.'

The caller replied, 'Have you anything better to go on?'

'Not yet. Wait until its dark so let's say ten o'clock tonight. I'll pay you when I know he's there.'

'Fine by me. I'll meet you outside Finsbury Park station.'

***

Rico arrived at Finsbury Park at 9.45 and stood outside the station. The middle aged looking man who approached him was small and thin and looked around nervously.

'Are you Rico?'

'Yeah, that's me. Was it you who called me?'

'Yes I'm Don. It's this way.'

As they walked, the man said, 'You'd better pay me for this because I know who you are.'

120

Rico nodded and pulled a fat envelope out of his pocket. 'It's all here but I need to know he's where you say he is. I'll pay you when I come out.'

'Okay, I'll be waiting.'

They arrived at a nondescript apartment block and the man pointed to an upper floor. 'That's where he is. Fourth floor, number 410.'

Rico whispered, 'Let's check the back just in case he has another way out.' He led the way round to a litter-strewn alleyway and heard the crunch of broken glass as they made their way towards a door set into the building. It was a fire door that could only be opened from the inside. It was just what he needed. 'Okay, let's go back to the front.'

The man turned to retrace his steps and Rico punched him hard in the back of the head before bringing out his knife. As the young man staggered, Rico plunged the knife deep into his side and watched as his victim fell silently to the ground. Rico rolled his body behind a large waste skip before walking back to the front of the building. He entered through the main door and made his way to the fourth floor. Number 410 was at the end of a narrow corridor and he approached it and rang the bell.

'Who is it?'

'It's next door. There's gas. You need to get out.'

The door opened a few inches and Rico threw his full weight at it. The door hit Frank straight in the face and Rico watched him stagger backwards and fall on his back. Rico charged in and kicked Frank hard in the ribs. As he lay winded, Rico knelt down on Frank's chest and heard him croak, 'What the fuck do you want?'

'What the fuck do you think. Where's the fentanyl?'

'Never got it. Don't know.' Rico pressed harder on his chest and Frank began to gasp for breath. 'Somebody switched cars. I don't know where it is.'

'Last chance, Frank.' He brought out the knife and extended the razor-sharp blade. As he touched Frank's throat he asked, 'Which way would you like it cut?'

'Okay, okay. It's in the rucksack behind you. Just take it.'

Without taking his eyes off him, Rico felt at his back and brought the rucksack into his sight. He began throwing the contents onto the floor. He came to the money and what was left of the fentanyl.

'There's some missing, Frank.'

'Maybe, but you've got the money too, so fuck off.'

Rico released his knee before bringing the knife deep across Frank's throat. Left to right. He jumped back as the dark arterial blood shot out and covered the TV screen in the corner. Rico walked through to the kitchen and found a supermarket plastic bag and placed the money and the fentanyl inside. Wiping the knife blade on a towel hanging on the wall he retracted the blade and shoved the knife in his pocket. Letting his eyes sweep round the room to check he'd left nothing behind he noticed Frank's mobile on the floor and picked it up and placed it in the bag. After wiping the door handle with his handkerchief he let himself out and walked quickly down the corridor towards the ground floor and the rear fire exit. Pushing the bar down he heard no alarm and walked out into the back alley without glancing at the skip.

Within five minutes he was on Seven Sisters Road and he walked for twenty minutes before flagging down a black cab. As he sat back in the taxi he thought of who he could sell the remaining fentanyl to. He brought Frank's phone from the bag and began scrolling through his contacts. If it came to it, he'd rather be caught at customs with a lot of money than a half a kilo of fentanyl and he needed the cash. He stopped the cab half a mile from his hotel and paid it off. When he reached his room he began making calls on Frank's phone.

***

The weekend weather forecast predicted 23C and full sun for southern England. Charlie knew it was good news for the organisers of the party. It would also reduce any resistance to his asking price. He had sold over three quarters of the coke and had a few dealers still to contact. As he made the round of calls and agreed meeting places and times he knew he would sell all his stock. An hour later he'd sold every bag and went through to his bedroom to pack an overnight bag. The small hotel near Burford was expecting him and he had a day before the rave to meet the dealers and collect the cash. It was his biggest ever rave and he knew it would lead to even bigger things. He threw his bags into the back of his black Range Rover Sport and headed west out of London towards the Marylebone Flyover and the M40 motorway.

Chapter Thirty-Three

It was a tight fit, but Jack had managed to store most of his files and office paraphernalia into the spare bedroom of his apartment. As he surveyed the boxes stacked on top of each other he felt relief and a little sadness at leaving his office in Kensington. His business had grown but not as quickly as the rents in west London. His new office was now his living room and he set up his laptop on the dining table. It was catch-up time after the move and he needed to get up to speed on various assignments he was working on. As he completed an invoice to a car dealership in Paddington who had hired him to produce evidence of fraud on the part of several employees, his mobile rang. There was a pause before the voice said, 'It's Tony.'

'Hi, Tony. How are you?'

'I'm okay, but I've had a phone call you need to know about. Some guy tried to sell me some cocaine. Said I'd bought before from a friend of his. I played him along because I thought it must be connected to the stuff that killed Rebecca. I said I was interested and would like to meet up.'

Jack felt his body stiffen. 'What did he sound like?'

'His English was broken. From my conversations at work, I'd say Spanish.'

'This is probably the guy we are looking for. Don't do anything, but when he rings again, say you're getting the money together. Text me his number so we both have it. I'll call you in an hour.'

Jack felt the excitement course through him. The text came through from Tony with the phone number. He went to his small drinks cabinet and brought out his prized bottle of Macallan 12-year-old. Pouring out a generous measure, he sat down and started to map out a plan.

***

Charlie spent two hours on his phone and double checked the times of meet-ups with dealers for the next morning. He would be stationed in a lay-by near the party site and there was no CCTV to worry about. He spaced each buyer out to make sure there was no contact between them and estimated he'd be on his way back to London by five o'clock in the afternoon. He went down for dinner and ordered a half bottle of Pinot Noir to go with his steak. No one took much notice of him and he was happy with that. In fact, he was happy with just about everything and he ordered a brandy to go with his coffee.

Next morning he rose at six and showered and shaved before going down for breakfast. Checking out at seven he paid in cash and took his cases out to his vehicle. It was exactly seven-thirty when he pulled into the lay-by and was pleased to see that all the overnight lorries had left.

There was a screening of trees between him and the road and passing vehicles would be none the wiser of the goings on. Pulling up to the far end, he parked and waited. He was determined to make each transaction happen quickly and there would be no testing. The buyers would just have to take his word they were getting high-grade cocaine. Anyway, where else could they buy at such short notice.

His first buyer arrived at eight and was happy to pay, take his bags and drive away. Other customers arrived at fifteen-minute intervals as instructed and at two o'clock he watched in his rear-view mirror as the last customer drew up behind his vehicle.

As Charlie drove back towards the motorway, he stopped at a small country pub and ordered pie and mash with gravy and a pint of locally-brewed ale. It was one of the finest meals he could remember. By 6pm he was back home in London and he began unpacking before heading for the shower. Life was sweet.

Chapter Thirty-Four

Jack rang Tony at work next morning.

'I've had the mobile number checked and it's a pay-as-you-go. The number is blocked and untraceable. Can I meet you, because we need a plan in case he calls again. How about one o'clock?'

'One is fine. See you then.'

Jack went through to his kitchen and brewed some coffee. It was strange not to be leaving for the office and he chuckled to himself. He thought of the hundreds of hours spent in London traffic just to go somewhere else to sit beside the same mobile phone. It all seemed madness to him now but he knew the kudos of having a Kensington address as he built his private investigation business. Sometimes he sat down in the evening and thought of the old days in the police force. He missed the camaraderie but he didn't miss the long and relatively low-paid hours. Being his own boss was liberating and he often thought he met a different type of criminal. He'd been shot at and stabbed and he had come through it all, but the scars were there both literally and metaphorically.

He poured his coffee into his favourite mug, rescued from the office, and walked through to his living room and sat down in his easy chair. His caseload was dominated by the investigation into the deaths of Susan Long and Rebecca Jennings and he thought he was now making some real progress. The telephone caller to Tony was his best break yet.

He finished his coffee and picked up his phone. It was a sunny day in London and he'd take the Tube, then walk the last mile to Tony's office. Locking up, he walked down to ground level and turned left along Elgin Avenue towards Maida Vale Underground Station.

***

Rico was working his way down Frank's stored numbers and came to Charlie. The number had been called three times in the last week and Rico thought it had to be a drug connection. He rang it and the voice just said, 'Yes.'

'You don't know me but I'm Rico, Frank's brother and I have some stuff to sell.'

'You don't sound like his brother.'

Rico laughed. 'We have different fathers.'

'So, where's Frank?'

'He's visiting family in Spain and asked me to look after things for a few days. He said you may like buy some more stuff.'

'Look, I don't know who you are. Give me your number and I may get back to you.'

Rico thought about it for a moment and knowing Charlie had heard of Frank, asked, 'Have you dealt with us before?'

There was a pause and Charlie replied, 'Maybe yes, maybe no. Ask your brother.'

Rico answered, 'I'll give you my number, but call me on it in the next seven days as it won't work after that.'

Rico carried on calling Frank's stored numbers but only found what he realised were small time street dealers. He needed to shift a lot of the fentanyl quickly and get back to Spain. Frank's body was bound to be found in the next couple of days if only because of the smell. He checked back on his notes and saw a cross he had made next to Charlie's name. He had made so many calls he couldn't remember making the mark but he underlined the name and added it to his list of priority contacts. As he looked around his small hotel room he realised his empire was at an end for the moment. He'd put too much trust in others and paid dearly for it. He'd find everyone who'd betrayed him and there would be no mercy. He gave himself a deadline of seventy-two hours to sell the last of the fentanyl and then he'd get back to Spain and re-group.

***

Charlie was taking a lot of calls from dealers involved with the free party. Every request was the same. 'I need more coke. Things are going mad and I can take anything you have. Top money is not a problem.'

His answer to each caller was the same, 'I'm back in London and don't have any stuff left. If I manage to get some more, it would be too late for the weekend wouldn't it?' Some of the dealers said they'd pay to have anything couriered out to them and Charlie said he'd get back to them if he was re-supplied.

***

Locals in Burford noticed unfamiliar vehicles beginning to arrive in the main street late on Saturday afternoon. Some were double parked outside the few small supermarkets and off-licence shops and others were congregating in the town's car park as if waiting for something to happen. The ATMs were being heavily used, with long queues forming as the town became busier. As early evening approached, vehicles of all shapes and sizes began arriving, then heading out of town and at one stage there was a group of young people trying to hitch lifts from passing cars. One local walking home from her trip to the shops was overheard saying, 'Lovely to see so many young people in the town. Must be a big birthday party or something.'

Five miles west of the town, the small B roads began to become congested as vehicles were parked on verges. By seven, vehicles were being dumped haphazardly in any patch of ground available and as gridlock approached there was no way in or out of the area except by foot. The music began at eight and for those still arriving, it acted as a beacon. Police had been alerted, but by the time they could allocate resources there was little they could do to stop the event. There was no way in for any vehicle. As the music boomed out and the complaints poured into the local police station, the inhabitants of Burford and surrounding areas knew they were in for a sleepless night.

Richard and his friends Mark and Rob had heard of the party through a friend and had made it to the field by coach and taxi from Oxford. They'd walked the last two miles through woodland, just following the sound of the music and other partygoers. They could hardly contain their excitement as they clumped through the downtrodden grass, each with a rucksack on their back. Richard had been to previous parties but his friends were first timers.

'The important thing is not to get split up.' Richard was going over the golden rules as they walked. 'It's usually difficult to get a signal on your phone as everyone else is trying to do the same. When we arrive we'll decide on a point to meet up should we become separated. There's often a totem pole type thing for that reason. Don't worry. The whole night will be brilliant.'

Twenty yards behind them three girls were keeping the boys in sight. Maggie was chatting to her friends, Sarah and Jess, as they walked.

'Let's just follow them,' Sarah said. 'They seem to know what they're doing.' They'd left Maggie's car in a piece of flattened ground at the edge of the wood and decided they'd use it for some sleep before driving back to Bristol the next day. It was their first ever free party. As the music became even louder they quickened their step and caught the boys up as the crowds became thicker. Richard turned and saw Maggie smile at him. He waved her over and all six were pushed together in the mass of bodies trying to make their way to the main party area. He shouted in her ear, 'I think there's more room if we try to move left towards those trees.'

Maggie shouted back, 'Okay. Let's go.'

They all pushed and shoved their way across towards a clump of trees and found a small piece of ground with no one standing on it. Richard shouted, 'This'll do.'

All the rucksacks were laid in a circle, introductions were bawled out and some hugging began. Richard pulled out a bottle of vodka from his rucksack and after taking a swig, offered it around. Jess had a bottle of Tequila and in ten minutes they were all passing bottles around. Jess started dancing and as the space began to shrink they all just ended up swaying to the music.

Richard had been away for about forty minutes and was grinning when he came back. In his absence they had all been drinking wine, tequila and vodka. The music had its own intoxication and as he sat down by a tree he shouted, 'Now the party begins.'

They watched as he brought two small plastic bags from his pocket. Examining both, he pushed one into the top pocket of his shirt and shook the other. He laughed as he delved into his rucksack and brought out a roadmap, laying it on his knees. Opening the packet, he spread white powder on the map and brought a ten-pound note from his trouser pocket. Using the edge of it he pushed some of the powder into three short lines before rolling the note up into a funnel. He bent down and snorted one of the lines. Maggie's face lit up and she took the rolled-up note from him and bent over the map. As she stood up she wiped her nostrils. Jess said, 'Me next' and squatted down to snort a line. Only Sarah moved back and shouted to Maggie, 'What are you doing?' Everyone was now laughing and dancing to the music as Richard brought out the second bag. He shouted, 'This is gonna be some night. Come on.'

The whole site was jumping and there were so many bodies in front of the stacked speakers, only swaying was possible. Girls sat on boys' shoulders and waved at the DJ. The generators worked overtime to keep the lighting and loudspeakers going. For first timers it was the most amazing night of their life. Freedom at last.

***

Jess needed to go to the toilet and turned to Sarah. She tried to say something and fell over onto the ground. No one saw her fall. As the music belted out over the field she became one of many lying prostrate and to on-lookers, probably just enjoying the atmosphere.

As midnight approached Richard began to gasp and as he tried to utter a shout, fell forwards. It was then that everyone saw Jess and in the dim light, her face was blue. Their screams went unnoticed and Maggie dropped to her knees and shouted at Jess to wake up. Mark saw Richard lying in the foetal position and immediately pushed his way towards him. The wall of noise stopped anyone from hearing the real shouts for help and panic set in around the base of the tree. Sarah punched 999 into her phone and waited. There was no signal. She re-tried and failed again to find reception. She looked down at Jess and knew she was dead. 'Oh, my God, no.' She looked across at Richard and saw his inert body. In the poor light she realised he was probably dead too. Turning to Maggie she held her and began weeping uncontrollably. And the music played on.

***

As reports filtered in on the possibility of drug overdoses, police and first responders eventually managed to enter the main arena at 1am. Although resuscitation had been performed on two partygoers it was believed that both were dead. Ten other partygoers had been admitted to the John Radcliffe Hospital in Oxford with what was thought to be drug-related conditions. Three were said to be in a life-threatening condition.

A silence descended on the party site as the police arrived and word of the deaths got round. By five, most of the partygoers and cars had gone and all that was left was a sea of litter. Police questioned the DJ and techies who were dismantling the sound stacks.

As the sun began to rise, Maggie and Sarah were in Burford waiting for Maggie's parents to arrive.

Mark and Rob were still at the police station giving statements. They said they had no idea where the drugs had come from and the only person who did know was dead. They were crying as the interview ended.

Chapter Thirty-Five

Charlie switched on the radio next morning and listened in horror as the headline news story told of the drug-related deaths of two young people at a free party in Oxfordshire. Ten others were in hospital with three of them on life support. The report went on to tell of the police enquiries to try and establish the source of the drugs. Names of the deceased were being withheld until next of kin had been informed and Charlie slumped in his chair as the realisation hit him that he could be responsible for the deaths. He knew a trail could be established back to him and his head jerked up as a police car with siren blaring shot past on the road outside his flat.

Thoughts tumbled through his mind and he knew it wasn't necessarily his cocaine that had been responsible for the tragedy and there could have been many dealers and sellers involved in a party of that magnitude. He sat and contemplated what he should do. If it had been his cocaine that had wreaked such havoc then he'd been scammed. He felt the anger rising within him and after half an hour he knew he had to do something. His thoughts went to the recent case of the death of a young woman in London and he remembered there was some sort of Spanish connection along the chain. He Googled the press reports of her death and began reading. His mouth went dry as he read of the presence of fentanyl in the supposed high-grade cocaine that had been bought. The boyfriend had thought there could be a Spanish connection in the drug chain after overhearing a telephone conversation, but police had been unable to verify this. Charlie remembered the mention of Spain when talking to Frank's brother when he'd called about him buying more cocaine.

He read on and wrote down Tony's place of work. Picking up his phone he rang the number for Screech Marketing.

'Tony Northwood please.'

'Who shall I say is calling?'

'It's private.'

When Tony answered, Charlie simply said, 'I think I can help you find who killed Rebecca.'

There was a pause. 'Who's calling?'

'My name is Charlie and I may have dealt with the man who sold you the drugs.'

'Can I get back to you on this number?'

'Yes, anytime.'

***

Tony looked at his watch. He realised he was due to meet Jack in an hour and made a note of Charlie's number.

Jack arrived just before one o'clock and they made their way to a nearby café. As they walked, Jack said, 'I've nothing of any great significance to report, I'm afraid.'

Tony replied, 'I have.'

They ordered a plate of sandwiches and two coffees and sat at a table near the back.

Tony looked at Jack and told him about the call he'd just received. 'The guy is most probably a dealer but he sounded as if he wanted to help. He may have thought he was selling high purity coke and didn't know all sorts of shit had been cut into it.'

'How did you leave it?'

'He said to call him back on the number he was phoning from.'

'How did he find you?'

'Didn't say, but my name and place of work have been splashed in the newspapers.'

Their sandwiches and coffees arrived and they stopped talking until the waitress moved away. Jack waited until Tony had taken a few bites and then said, 'It's the break we've been waiting for and you have to meet him. If we handle this right we find the guy who sold you the stuff that killed Rebecca.'

'I'm fine with that.'

'Don't forget there's danger involved, Tony.'

'I don't care. This is for Rebecca.'

Jack sipped his coffee but didn't eat. 'I'd like you to call him back and arrange a meeting. We need to know how much he is prepared to talk about, and specifically he needs to give up a name. He could get cold feet so we may only get one shot at it. I suspect he has a family and has a conscience about young people dying from adulterated drugs. It may seem strange to you but we are lucky to find someone like this in the drugs business. Let's go outside and call him. If he suggests meeting in a secluded area just say no. Suggest you meet in a car park somewhere and I will be close by. Daytime only and I'll be able to get some shots of him.'

They walked to where Jack had parked his car in a side street and Jack began to make some notes for Tony.

Ask his name.

Why is he helping you?

What name did the dealer give?

Does he know where the dealer lives?

Was there any mention of Spain?

What purity did the seller say the cocaine was?

Is he meeting the dealer again?

If he is, will he give you the details?

Jack handed the questions to Tony and waited while he read them. He looked up and asked, 'What if he refuses to answer them?'

'He may refuse some but I think he wants to talk. The most important questions are the last two. If we can bring him out into the open on those then we have a good chance of nailing the top man. My client is after the guy running the Spanish operation but if we can connect all the dots we may bring some closure to the families of the youngsters who died in Oxfordshire.'

Tony cleared his throat loudly and there was a small tremor in his hands as he punched the numbers. He put the phone on open.

'Hello, Charlie, it's Tony. You called me earlier about my girlfriend, Rebecca.'

'Hi, Tony. Yeah. I wanted to explain a few things.'

Tony immediately said, 'About why you are killing young people?'

Charlie coughed and said, 'Let me say a couple of things. I had no idea this would happen. I really didn't. I supply good quality cocaine to intelligent people every day and this is the first time I've heard of a death. It wasn't me who supplied you and I don't even know who was responsible for killing those people at the party. It may not have been me because there were lots of dealers involved. It's a long chain out of London. It's called County Lines.'

Anger welled up in Tony and Jack gave him a hand gesture to cool down. He pointed to the sheet of paper on Tony's lap.

'Look, I only know you as Charlie. Who are you?'

'Charlie is all you're going to get, so don't ask.'

'Why are you doing this?'

'I thought I was selling high-grade cocaine. Now I know different. I bought it quickly from a new dealer and I was scammed.'

'Who was the dealer?'

'Who knows?

'You must know something about him?'

'The first guy I dealt with called himself Frank but the guy who sold me the crap cocaine said his name was Rico. He was minding the shop during his brother's absence in Spain. Or so he said.' He saw Jack nodding as the Rico name was mentioned and realised it could be another piece in the puzzle.

Tony forgot the script and asked, 'Where can I find him?'

'Look, Tony, I can understand your anger.'

He didn't have time to finish before Tony shouted back, 'How the fuck would you understand anything? You're just a dope-dealing piece of scum.'

'Do you want my help or not?'

Tony went quiet and said, 'Yes.'

'Right, this guy has more stuff to sell and I have two days left to contact him. He probably doesn't know it was his stuff that caused the deaths at the party, as if he would care. For obvious reasons I can't contact the police but it would be an opportunity to bring the bastard out into the open.'

Tony turned to Jack and mouthed, 'What do I say?'

Jack scribbled, 'Tell him about me.'

Tony returned to the phone, 'I have a private investigator helping me. He'll get involved if you can set up a meeting with this Rico guy.'

There was a pause before Charlie said, 'That's okay by me but I don't want any police involvement. I'm going to stay in the background and leave it to you guys.'

'I have the PI with me here so I'll put you on open phone and maybe we can talk about how to do this.'

There was a moments silence before Charlie answered.

'Okay, let's do that. What's the investigator's name?'

Jack leaned across to the phone. 'I'm Jack Barclay. We really need to meet up and discuss this.'

'That's fine by me but just the three of us.'

Jack said, 'Of course. How about you contacting Rico to confirm you need more stuff quickly. Tell him you need two hundred grams to get his interest. He'll want to set the meeting place. Ring Tony back after you've spoken with him.'

Charlie replied, 'Okay, you'll hear from me.' The line went dead and Tony looked at Jack before saying, 'This had better work.'

'It will,' Jack said.

Chapter Thirty-Six

Charlie called Rico an hour later. 'You maybe won't remember me, but my name is Charlie. You called yesterday about a possible sale.'

'Who could forget a name like that?' Rico replied. 'How much Charlie are you looking for, Charlie?'

He'd heard the quip so many times before and let out a low groan. 'I need two hundred grams of best.'

'I can do that. It's a big order. You got a festival coming up?'

'Yeah, something like that. I'll pay good money for top grade.'

'It'll be the best and it's seventy pounds a bag.'

'Sixty and we're in business.'

'Sixty-five and that's it.'

'Okay, as long as it's the best.'

'Don't worry, it will be. I need a couple of days to get the stuff together. I'll get back to you late tomorrow to agree a place to meet up. Are you in London?'

'Yes.'

'Okay, I'll keep this number going. If anything changes, call me on it'

Charlie replied, 'We need to choose our meeting place well. I don't want any fuck-ups.'

'You think I do?'

Charlie heard the line go dead. All he wanted was the fentanyl out of the picture so he could get back to the business of dealing in the real stuff. He was only sorry he wouldn't be there to watch the deal go down.

Charlie punched in Tony's number and said, 'We're in business. Rico will call me late tomorrow to finalise details for the meeting. Call your private investigator and let's see if we can meet up after I get the call from Rico. Do you know what you will do when you meet this guy?'

'Ask Jack Barclay. He has spent a long time looking for the top guy in this operation. It'll be up to him to call the shots.'

Chapter Thirty-Seven

Jack was staying at Eva's place tonight and he thought about the day's events as he drove along the Embankment. He had no doubt that Charlie was the guy who had supplied the deadly cocaine for the party and he was taking a chance in getting in touch with Tony. It was almost as if his integrity as a reputable cocaine dealer to the young London middle class was at stake. He was passing Westminster Bridge when his mobile rang and he pressed 'open phone'.

'It's Matt. I thought you should know two bodies have been found just off Seven Sisters Road in Finsbury Park and it looks as if the deaths are connected. One male body was found stabbed behind a waste skip in a back alley and he's yet to be formally identified. The other was in a flat just opposite. The one inside had his throat cut we think about four days ago. Place stinks to high heaven. We've got some intel on him and it could be he is connected to drug distribution. His house was burnt down in Lewisham last week. Goes by the name of Frank Portman. Not his week, eh!'

Jack laughed at the cop black humour and said, 'I know the name from my investigations in Malaga. I may be able to help you on this, Matt but I need a couple of days.'

'No problem. It's another lowlife off the streets. Look after yourself.'

As he drove, he felt bad. Frank was the name of the dealer who met Tony. The guy who caused Rebecca's death. He could have levelled with Matt, but he needed to follow through and confront Rico. He called Eva and said he was fifteen minutes away.

'Dinner's ready,' she told him.

He'd bought a bottle of red wine from a small corner shop in Maida Vale and hoped it was good. He'd looked at their flowers and decided they were half dead. It was a risk too far. He found a parking space in the next road and walked back to Eva's. She was dressed in a cream-coloured dress, cut just above the knee and when she opened the door he couldn't see much else. Her beauty was intoxicating and as she stretched out her arms he leaned into her long kiss.

'Missed you so much, Jack.'

'Me too, honey. I think it's been two days but feels like two weeks. Are you going to let me in?'

They tumbled through the door, laughing and touching.

'I've cooked a chilli, Jack. Is that okay?'

They both started laughing again and Jack said, 'I've heard it's best to turn the oven right down and let it rest for about half an hour.'

'Who told you that?'

'I just made it up.'

'Well actually, I've heard the same. I'll just turn it down.'

Jack moved into the bedroom and Eva came in a minute later.

'God, Jack you look wonderful.'

All Jack saw was a blur of cream as her dress disappeared over her head. He lay on his back as she straddled him, moving slowly and rhythmically. She called his name out as they became lost in one another. Jack drew her head down and kissed her.

As they lay together afterwards Jack looked at Eva and whispered, 'We must try to take it a bit slower next time.'

'How about a re-run after dinner?' Eva pushed a strand of hair off Jack's forehead and said, 'I love you, Jack.'

'I love you too.'

They dressed before going through to the kitchen.

She asked, 'Hungry?'

'I seem to have worked up an appetite. How about you?'

'Ravenous.'

Eva poured out two glasses of the Shiraz Jack had brought and they clinked glasses.

Jack said, 'To us, Eva.'

He wakened to the sounds of the city as early morning commuters began their daily grind to work. His right arm had gone numb as he lay close to Eva and he gently pulled himself away before padding through to the kitchen to percolate some coffee.

Chapter Thirty-Eight

Rico tried not to get his hands dirty nowadays, but as he sat in his hotel room he thought of a night five years ago in Malaga. He'd just set up new heroin routes from Morocco and he needed to recoup the money he'd laid out to establish them. An investigator hired by a competitor was digging around to find out where he was operating from and soon the heat was endangering his fledgling operation, not to mention his reputation. Rico didn't hesitate and chose a night during the Feria de Día when noisy crowds thronged the streets. He posed as a dealer and lured the detective to an apartment in the La Palma district of the city with the promise of information on a drug boss who owed him a considerable amount of money. He'd insisted that no names were to be used and he refused to identify himself. The detective took the bait and arrived at the apartment just before 11pm. Rico had removed the light bulb in the stairwell and he emerged from the shadows as he saw the detective's eyes squinting in the semi-darkness. He despatched him in a matter of seconds with his stabbing knife and carried the body out to the alley running behind the apartment block. He rolled the body up in a carpet in the boot of his car. No one asked questions in that part of the city and the detective simply disappeared. No trace of him was ever found. Some said he was buried somewhere in the foothills of the Sierra Nevada, others thought he was feeding the fish at the bottom of the Mediterranean and Rico just listened to the rumours and shrugged. Things soon returned to normal for the criminals and drug dealers who enjoyed the good life on the Costa Del Sol.

Dealing with those who opposed him had never been a problem and he'd deal with the private detective who was trying to find him in London. He was the only possible obstacle to him recouping all his losses. No one would stop the deal with Charlie and it would get him back to Spain and the life he loved.

Chapter Thirty-Nine

Jack felt good as he left Eva's next morning. The sky was blue and there was a warmth to the early-morning October air. His phone rang as he headed west across the Embankment.

'Hi Matt, you're early.'

'You driving?'

'Yeah, but go ahead.'

'Tell you what, call me back when you're stationary.'

'What is it, Matt?'

'Jack, just call me when you land. Speak later.'

He knew it was bad. How bad, he'd know in about the twenty minutes it would take to arrive home. He felt his anxiety levels rise and tried to increase his speed, but the traffic was nose to tail. After another mile he spotted a hotel car park without a barrier and pulled in.

'It's Jack. What's happened?'

He heard Matt clear his throat. 'You've spent a lot of time in Eva Long's company and there's no easy way of saying this, Jack. We have reason to believe that Eva may be involved in her sister's activities. Maybe her death.'

Jack sat without moving and tried to take in what he had just heard.

'You're wrong, Matt. So fucking wrong. Where did you get this from?'

'You know I can't say, Jack and I'm really sorry. There's a new line of enquiry and it includes Eva. I only tell you this as a friend and you can't say anything, least of all to Eva. I need to meet you privately.'

Jack fell completely silent as he listened to his old police chum.

'Okay, Matt. Thank you for the call. There must be a huge mistake. How sure are you?'

There was a pause and Matt said, 'That's why I need to speak to you.'

Jack's voice wavered as he asked, 'When can we meet?'

'I'm committed all day today. I'll ring you early evening. And Jack, you know how really sorry I am to give you this news.'

'I know. Thanks.'

Jack sat motionless as his mind swirled. 'Oh, God, let this not be true.'

He exhaled deeply before pulling out of the car park and continuing his journey home. He was driving faster than usual and taking chances as he became vaguely aware of other drivers blasting their horns at him. As he threaded his way through Earls Court his mind went back to the time he served in the police and found himself the victim of a smear campaign orchestrated by the brother of a villain he had arrested for dealing drugs in east London. The campaign of innuendo against him had been brutal, with rumours swirling around that Jack had planted class A drugs in the victim's home during the arrest. Some of Jack's colleagues on the force who were aware of his success rate when it came to nailing career criminals were slow in coming forward to defend his character. Jack found himself in the position of not knowing who to trust and his job became almost untenable as the underworld saw a chance to fan the flames of doubt as to the integrity of the police. The more he denied any involvement the worse the situation became. The whole campaign against him came crashing down when the dealer's brother was overheard bragging in a pub about how easy it was to frame a copper. Two of the guys on the next table were off-duty police and within hours the brother had been arrested. Jack had found out who his real friends were but the damage to his reputation was permanent. As the months rolled on he realised his career had stalled although no reason was ever given. He had always been scrupulous about his conduct in the force and the continued suspicion surrounding him led to his decision to retire early. He jumped as a police car with its siren screaming edged past and it took him out of his reverie.

As he approached his street he checked his watch. 9am. He switched off his phone. Eva would be at the office now and he needed to have some time to go over things in his mind. Flopping down on his sofa he began thinking back to all the situations he'd been in since taking on the case. He couldn't remember one time when he'd had suspicions about Eva's conversations or actions. In all the time they'd spent together she would have slipped up at least once if she was hiding anything.

He went to the kitchen to make some coffee and tried to hold back his anger. Someone was trying to muddy the waters here and as he poured coffee into his mug he realised he was fighting on several fronts. Susan was dead, Rebecca was dead and now Eva was under suspicion. He sat down and thought back to his time in Malaga. It had to do with their time there and he began making notes for his conversation with Matt later in the day. He knew Matt wouldn't be able to say too much but perhaps he could ask him obliquely how Eva was suddenly in the frame. He switched his phone on and there was a message from her. 'Hi, my love. Call me when you can.'

He switched the phone off again and closed his eyes. As his mind raced, he tried to think of those who wanted her implicated in the murder of her twin sister. The list grew in his mind and he realised that everyone inside the drug cartel had an agenda to push. He had to find the one with the most compelling reason.

Chapter Forty

Rico began researching possible meeting places. He knew the problem was CCTV. London was swamped with cameras and he needed to be totally alone with Charlie for the deal. He began thinking about venues that would afford him some protection from unwanted intrusions and began by looking at empty office blocks and warehouse buildings coming up for sale or auction. As he brought the photos up on screen he soon realised they were all heavily guarded with high fencing and security cameras. He had no idea of the alarm systems in place but he knew there would be plenty. Sitting back, he closed his eyes and thought of the ideal situation for the meeting. If it was a place where Charlie felt relaxed and safe it would be helpful. Maybe somewhere with distractions. An exclusive address where most people could only dream of. He let his thoughts drift and pictured a penthouse apartment with a view over London and some relaxing music in the background. For what he had in mind this would be the ideal scenario and he began researching websites offering the accommodation he was looking for.

After half an hour's surfing the web he hit on a company offering private luxury apartments in west London with various service packages. Hire periods were from three hours to a time to be agreed, with absolute discretion assured. Rico phoned the company and a cultured female voice answered, 'London Elite.'

Rico asked, 'Do you have any suites available at short notice?'

'Let me check for you. We have a lovely suite in Mayfair available, sir. When would you be looking to hire it?'

'I need it in two days' time from four in the afternoon until seven.'

'We could arrange that, sir. Would you like some details emailed to you?'

'No, it sounds like what I'm looking for. If you can give me your address I'll come in tomorrow and pay cash for the rental.'

'That will not be a problem, sir. You can come and go as you wish in total privacy.'

'Excellent. My name is Francisco. I'll see you tomorrow.'

'I'll keep the room provisionally booked until then and we look forward to seeing you, sir.'

Rico sat back and began to think out his plan. His shopping list would take him most of tomorrow morning to complete and when he'd finished writing it he picked up his phone and made a reservation with Iberia on the last flight out of Heathrow to Malaga on Thursday night.

He called Charlie back. 'It's Rico. I'm getting the stuff ready for you now. We'll meet in central London on Thursday afternoon and I'll call you in the late morning on the day to confirm the venue. I want the cash in fifties and remember, only you.'

'I understand and I'll have the cash. I'll wait for your call. See you Thursday.'

***

Charlie put a call into Tony. 'I've just heard from Rico and he wants the deal done late afternoon Thursday. Don't know the venue but it'll be central London and he'll let me know about two hours before. Can you update your detective friend?'

'Yes, I'll call him now. Will you have all the cash by then?'

Charlie replied, 'That's all fixed. Could you get Jack to call me as there are one or two things we need to go over.'

'Yes, no problem. We need to meet up tomorrow morning.'

'I'll wait to hear from you, Tony.'

Chapter Forty-One

As Jack went over past events in his mind, the person who had suffered the most in Spain was Vicente. He'd lost his livelihood, his status, his lifestyle and he knew he was always going to on the mob's hit list. What he had said to the Spanish police in the hope of receiving a lighter sentence was known only to a few, but he could have thrown suspicion on anyone as his interrogation went on. This looked like revenge served up by a man who knew his life had been destroyed and for all Jack knew, his own name could have been called into doubt. What he had to do was find out if Eva would be the subject of an investigation. How substantial were the accusations? He put a call into Matt and it went straight to message. 'It's Jack. Can you give me a call when possible? Thanks.'

He felt a little better having thought it through and called Eva. 'Hi, it's Jack. Got your message. Speak later.' As he sipped his coffee he decided to say nothing to Eva until he found the source of the accusation. After what she'd been through this would devastate her and everything in his being told him it was a lie. He made a mental note to go through the chain of events involving Vicente when he spoke with Matt. He might even persuade him to allow a meeting with the officer in charge of the case.

He opened his laptop and began drafting a document outlining all that had happened during his time in southern Spain. He named meeting places, restaurants, bars and hotels with dates and times where possible to allow verification checks to be made if necessary. Paying particular attention to Vicente he detailed the trap set by the Spanish police and the recovery of the drug money. As he typed, he made it quite clear that he was the one person who had been instrumental in capturing Vicente with enough evidence to prosecute. He presumed the police knew this but perhaps they weren't fully aware of his relationship with Eva. He had to make sure they knew everything. During his professional life he had spent thousands of hours listening to others telling lies or at least being economical with the truth and this case was no different, except it was personal. The old mantra from his time in the police came to mind:

ABC

Assume nothing
Believe no one
Challenge everything

He would do all those things and more to clear Eva's name.

***

Jack, Charlie and Tony met at 9.00 the next morning in a small café in Paddington. Jack was first to arrive and chose a table at the back, slightly apart from other breakfast diners. It wasn't exactly a greasy spoon place but it was unpretentious and Jack hoped the three of them would not be of any particular interest to locals. Charlie and Tony arrived within a few minutes of one another and they all ordered off the simple breakfast menu.

Jack started the conversation after they had all begun eating and said, 'This could be one of the more unusual breakfast meetings you'll ever have, but we need a plan of action. It's a disadvantage not to know the type of setting he is going to choose, but once we do know we can adapt our approach.'

Charlie spoke up and said, 'Much will depend on whether he really is on his own or has back-up with him. We agreed we'd both be on our own, but who knows?'

Tony remained silent and concentrated on eating his scrambled egg as Jack spoke up again. Looking at Charlie he said, 'I'm going to assume the worst possible scenario – and that is Rico being armed, taking your money and keeping the cocaine.'

'And what if that does happen?'

'Just let him try that and I'll take it from there.'

'Yeah, but what about me? He knows I've seen him. Where will you be?'

'Closer than you think. I'll have your back, Charlie.'

'I don't like it. I don't like it at all.'

Tony chipped in, 'We can't legislate for every little move.'

'It's okay for you to say that.' Charlie pushed his plate away from him and stared hard at Jack. 'Have you ever been in situations like this before?'

'As a matter of fact, I have and worse. I'm still here and you will be too.'

'Will you be armed?'

'All you need to know is that I'll be ready.' Charlie sank back in his seat and said nothing as Jack continued talking. 'The venue could be some deserted piece of land but there are few of those in

London now. It could take place inside a building, but if it's central London as he says, he has limited means of leaving un-noticed no matter how he is travelling.' He asked Charlie, 'How will you carry the money?'

'In the rucksack and I'll have a testing kit for the cocaine. He'll want to check my banknotes. Won't be a problem. In the end we'll probably just swap bags. To be honest, I've never been involved in anything like this before, but I want to get this bastard.'

Tony turned to Charlie and said, 'Not as much as I do.'

Jack drained his coffee and looked at them both in turn.

'It's going to be dangerous and we all know it. All I want to say to you is that if the deal goes down okay he'll be captured on the way out. If he cuts up rough there will be immediate back-up to help you, Charlie. I can't promise anymore.'

Tony stared at Jack and said, 'Where do I fit in?'

'You can't be there, but I'll make sure you know everything that goes down.'

Charlie pushed his chair back and said, 'I can't do it. This guy is calling all the shots and I'm just walking into God knows what.'

Jack signalled to Charlie to sit down again. 'It's because of you we're sitting here. Don't expect any sympathy from me. It's the fact that you are willing to try and nail the boss of this cartel that I'm even prepared to sit at the same table. It's a small redeeming gesture from you and your detestable way of life.'

Charlie looked down as Jack finished and shook his head.

Jack asked, 'In or out, Charlie?'

There was a pause before he looked up and said, 'Out.'

'You definitely don't want to be involved?'

'No. Too many unknowns. I supply middle-class people with a plant-based substance to enhance their weekends. It's usually harmless fun. I'm not a gangster.'

Tony banged the palm of his hand on the table. 'How can you sit there and say that? It's because of you and people like you that Rebecca is dead. A dreadful death.'

Charlie leaned back when Tony balled his fist. Jack placed his hand on Tony's arm to prevent him making contact.

'I know how you must feel and I agree with you, but we have a job to do here to get Rico off the streets.' Tony relaxed his body as he slumped in his chair. Nearby diners tried to avoid eye contact with them as Jack said quietly, 'Okay. We move to plan B.'

Tony looked puzzled. 'And what's that?'

Jack laid his hands palm down on the table and said, 'I'll do it.'

Tony interrupted and said, 'But he knows you.'

'True, we met at Rebecca's funeral but I was diving for his ankles and he never got a proper look at me. If he's tried to find any image of me then he would have probably failed. It'll be okay. Charlie, you will continue to be the contact for Rico and wait for him to call you with the time and place. Have the money ready and packed and I'll collect it from you in the morning. Call me as soon as you hear from him.'

'So, I just hand you the money and hope everything works out?'

Jack could hardly contain his anger any longer and said, 'You make your money from other people's misery. Either trust me or do the deal yourself. There is another option if you don't help me.'

'And what's that?'

'I turn you in.'

Charlie glowered then asked, 'Why the big interest on your part?'

'It's personal, but we've got to get him. I'll do the deal myself.' He turned to Tony and said, 'I'll call you when it's over. I hope I can get you some closure for Rebecca.'

As Charlie rose from the table he looked down at Jack and said, 'Good luck. I'll see you in the morning.'

Jack didn't move. 'Pay the breakfast bill on your way out.'

Chapter Forty-Two

Jack brewed some coffee and opened up his laptop. He hadn't heard from Eva and felt anxious. An update from Matt would help. His call came just after 7pm.

'Hi, Jack and sorry to be so late. It's been a hell of a day. There's been another death as a result of the drugs sold at the party in Oxfordshire. The girl was only seventeen and she's the daughter of a cabinet minister. You can't believe the shit that's coming down on us. It's mental. Fentanyl again and there's still three others in comas at the hospital and they're not looking good. This will be tomorrow's headlines, that's for sure. This fentanyl stuff is bloody lethal. It's taken the death of a politician's daughter to ram home the new dangers to our youngsters.'

Jack listened and waited as Matt talked on.

'There are so many users now and it's become a dealer's paradise. Trouble is, no one knows what they're buying. If it's top grade it can be lethal and if its rubbish with opioids cut in then it's definitely a killer. London's awash with the stuff and the prices are going down so the dealers are moving out into the country. We've got kids selling to kids and for the most part their parents don't even know it's happening. It's frightening. There are no easy answers to it except try to nail those at the top of the distribution chains. Trouble is finding them with any evidence to go on.'

'That's what I need to speak to you about, Matt, but I need your help. Is this line secure?'

'Should be as far as my phone is concerned. Don't know about yours.'

'I really need to meet up with you but we are running out of time.'

'Running out of time for what?'

'I'm meeting Rico tomorrow, the guy who supplied the fentanyl.'

There was a pause then, 'Jesus, you can't do this on your own. We need to be involved. This is what we've been waiting for.'

'Right now, that's the way it's going down, but I need to get Rico for another reason.'

'What do you mean?'

'It's Eva. I know she never had anything to do with Susan's life in Spain or any of her friends. Someone is putting the shade on her and I think I know who that is. I need your help to expose him. It's all about the arrests in Malaga and revenge.'

'Look, Jack, I'll see what I can do, but I need to know about your meeting with Rico.'

'Matt, we've known each other for a long time and believe me I know you can try harder than that. I want you to be able to call me and say the accusations against Eva are untrue. You have your priorities and I have mine.'

Matt asked, 'Where are you meeting him?'

'He won't say until two hours before the meeting.'

'What's going down?'

'Crap cocaine probably cut with fentanyl.'

'Jesus, Jack we need to be in on this and I can go official if I have to.'

'Yes, you do that and completely fuck things up. I'm going to need some help, that's for sure, but you make that call to find the source on the slur against Eva and we can talk again.'

'Give me a couple of hours and I'll come back to you.'

Jack put a call into Eva immediately after the call ended. 'Hi, it's me. Sorry for the silence today. How are you?'

'Jack, I've been worried. Are you alright?'

'Yes, everything is fine, just very busy. Things are developing and tomorrow will be busy too. How about you?'

'It's been a hectic day, too. Ten minutes for lunch. Anyway, good to know you are making progress.'

'We may be closing in on the drug gang that Susan became involved with in Spain. I'm working with the police, so please don't worry.'

'It all sounds a bit scary, Jack. When can we meet up? I've got another couple of very busy days but maybe you could come over Friday or I could come to you for a change?'

'Friday sounds great. But we can talk before then. Let's make it my place and I'll cook something Spanish.'

'Brilliant. I can't wait, Jack. I really can't.'

'I'll call you tomorrow, Eva. Love you.'

'Love you. Bye.'

He poured himself a whisky and sat down to wait for the call from Matt. By the sound of things, Matt needed him more than the other way round, but he knew he'd need back-up tomorrow. It all depended on the location for the deal and there wouldn't be much time to agree tactics. As he sat waiting, he knew that Rico was almost bound to be armed and he couldn't match that. Matt must have thought that out as well. He nursed his drink and waited for the call.

Chapter Forty-Three

Rico woke early and showered. He left the hotel at seven-thirty and mixed with the early-morning London commuters as he made his way towards a café near Victoria Station he'd seen the previous day. Ordering toast and coffee, he pulled out the list from his pocket:

Serrated knife

Zip ties

Duct tape

Rucksack

As he looked out onto the early morning street scene, with café and restaurant deliveries being made through the throng of people walking to work, he pulled out his phone to find the nearest stockist of these everyday items. His shortlist took his mind back to his first ever robbery in Malaga when he was still a teenager. The small supermarket he had chosen was close to villas and apartments frequented by tourists from the UK and northern Europe. He had noticed how many of them used cash for their purchases and as they stocked up on booze, the till was usually stuffed with notes every night. He'd waited until 10 o'clock one Saturday night and entered the store just as the owner was about to lock up. The lights had been switched off at the front to discourage late shoppers and Rico pulled the knife on him when he saw the owner start to flick the lights off in the display cabinets. He was ready for some resistance and when the owner began trying to punch Rico, he flicked the blade of the knife into his cheek and pulled a long zip tie from his pocket. As the owner realised he could not react, he stopped struggling, blood running into his mouth. Rico threatened him again before dragging him behind the counter. The till popped open and Rico grabbed all the notes. He was outside with the takings in two minutes and all the blurred CCTV camera picked up was a figure thought to be male, wearing leather motor cycle gear and a black crash helmet. Over the months, he raided five other small supermarkets in and around Torremolinos and Benalmadena, always using the same tried and tested tactics. His getaways were always on a scooter stolen within an hour of the raid and he knew the use of the knife was the key to his successes. After he drew blood, he was never challenged by anyone who happened to be in the supermarket. As his notoriety grew he became known as the supermarket slasher and the nickname only served to increase fear and make each raid easier.

Rico didn't blow the money. Instead, he invested in the most lucrative business ever to hit the Costa Del Sol since the early days of the tourist invasion. The takings stolen from the supermarkets allowed him to buy his way into the drugs business and after the robberies he had been able to set himself up as a wholesale supplier of cocaine to the rich and famous. Spending his immense new wealth quietly but wisely, he built up a portfolio of property he let out in the area around Puerto Banús. Within three years he was the undisputed king of coke in Marbella. When any young pretenders strayed into his turf, the full might of his organisation came down on them and the threat was usually crushed in days. Rico never forgot the thrill he experienced when he drew the knife on that first shopkeeper all those years ago and unbeknown to his lieutenants he sometimes went out very late at night and dealt with transgressors personally. On every occasion they were never heard of again.

As his organisation grew, he stepped back and went into semi-retirement with an import business in rattan patio furniture as a cover for his immense wealth. His days were spent on the golf course and his generosity in helping fund improvements around the course soon found him being appointed club captain. With his newly built luxury villa and legendary pool parties, he'd made all his dreams come true.

Chapter Forty-Four

Matt's call came at eight am and Jack was already showered and drinking coffee in the kitchen.

'Hi, Matt. I'm just watching the news and you were right about the headlines. She was so young. Tragic.'

'Jack, the shit is still pouring down on us from the top. Do you have anything more for me since we spoke last night?'

'No, nothing. Do you?'

'Yes. I've spoken with my counterpart in Malaga and filled him in. This is totally off the record.'

'Of course.'

'The accusation has come from Vicente Perez, who was offering information in return for a lighter sentence. He was not specific about Eva and nothing he said has yet been corroborated. He was spewing out all sorts of accusations over many interviews but there are numerous inconsistencies in his version of events. They are still investigating whether Eva is connected to any of the activities of the cartel.'

Jack asked, 'So where does that leave her when she returns to Spain to help clear her sister's villa?'

'It could mean she is interviewed.'

'You mean arrested?'

'No, just questioned. There's no evidence yet that she was involved in anything to do with her sister's activities and that's all I know at the moment.'

Jack waited for a moment before asking, 'Why would she come to me in the first place and ask for help if she was involved? It doesn't make any sense.'

'I know, but the Spanish police have to follow up the accusation. They have no choice. I've asked to be kept in the loop and if there are any developments, you will be the first to know. I'm sorry, Jack. I really am.'

'I'll call you in the morning, Matt. I have no idea when Rico will make his move but at the moment I'm down to meet him on my own. I'm going to stand in for Charlie.'

'Will you have the money with you?'

'I'm meeting Charlie first thing and I'll have it all in a rucksack.'

'Christ, Jack you can't do this on your own. He's bound to be armed. You won't stand a chance. You need us in on this.'

'I know. As soon as we have the location from him I'll call you.'

'I'm going to set the team up tonight, Jack. We'll be ready when you call us.'

'Okay. We'll talk when I have the location. Speak later.'

***

It was dark as Charlie let himself into his London apartment at nine o'clock. He'd stopped off for a drink at his local to relax after his meeting. He poured himself a Scotch and slumped in his favourite armchair. The soft night thrum of black cabs from nearby Marylebone High Street was reassuring as he sipped his drink. As he thought of tomorrow, he knew his money would be at risk. He would load fifties in wads at the top and hope Rico didn't use a note counter all the way down. If necessary, Jack would just have to blag it with Rico as the exchange took place. It was going to be street-level cocaine at the best with the likelihood of other rubbish cut in. All he wanted was this Rico guy to be taken off the streets with his fentanyl so he could get back to his civilised cocaine business. Jack seemed the ideal guy to see it through. He finished his drink and went through to his study to sort out the contents of the rucksack.

Chapter Forty-Five

London woke up to another clear blue sky and commuters seemed a little happier as the early morning sun warmed the city. Jack rose at six and percolated some coffee before showering. He had slept fitfully and during his waking moments had tried to guess the possible scenarios for his meeting with Rico. He'd need back-up, but not knowing the location was a big handicap. If the meeting was to be outdoors, then Matt's promise of support would be slightly easier to put in place. With the latest high-profile death as a result of fentanyl at the rave in Oxfordshire he knew there would be no expense spared in terms of resource from the police. Rico would receive a head shot the moment it looked as if he was about to use a firearm or knife. As he drank his coffee he wondered if Rico would choose a different venue. Maybe somewhere inside. Somewhere much more difficult to manage. One thing was for sure and that was Charlie wouldn't see his money again. At worst it would leave with Rico and at best be confiscated by the police. His mobile rang and he walked across the kitchen to answer it.

Matt's voice sounded tired. 'Morning, Jack. I hope you slept better than me.'

'Nope, too much going on.'

'Have you heard anything from Rico?'

'Not a word. He's going to keep everything to the last minute. Makes it difficult for me to prepare.'

'That's why I'm phoning you. I've got the green light for as many people as I need, but I'm worried for you. Would Rico know you up close?'

'Maybe not, but I can see where you're going with this. I'm determined to go ahead with this wherever he decides to meet. I know the risks.'

'You can't be sure if Charlie will actually supply the money. Maybe he has another agenda. There are too many unknowns, Jack. Why don't you let us handle it?'

'I'm going to see this through, Matt. As soon as I know the where and when then I'll call you. We should have a couple of hours' notice. I'm leaving soon to meet Charlie and collect the money and testing kit. I'll call you after that.'

'Okay, Jack but think on what I've said.'

'I will. Speak later.'

A few minutes later Charlie called. 'I've prepared the rucksack. It's all there.'

'So where do you want to meet me?'

There's a big green DIY store on the Finchley Road with a clock on the front of the building. It has a car park at the back.'

'I know it.'

'I'm in a blue Mercedes M Class. What will you be in?'

'A black SAAB 900.'

'Right, I'll see you there at 11.00.'

***

Jack arrived in the car park a few minutes before eleven and parked up near the back where there were plenty of empty bays. He spotted Charlie's blue Mercedes coming through the entrance at ten past eleven. It pulled up next to him and Charlie peered over before opening his window. He gestured for Jack to come round to the front passenger door of his vehicle.

Jack climbed out and walked round to the Mercedes. He noticed the tension in Charlie's face as he settled into the seat and waited for Charlie to say something.

'So, it's just you meeting him. No police involvement.'

'It's just me and him.'

'You don't look a lot like me.'

'He's never met you.'

Charlie looked out as if checking the car park. 'You must really want this guy.'

'I need him to clear up a misunderstanding about a friend of mine.'

'Is that it?'

'No. I think he has a large supply of fentanyl and I want it off the streets, if only for Rebecca.'

'What happens if he just tries to take the money?'

'He can try. It'll be one on one. I've been there before and I'm still here talking to you.'

Charlie passed him the rucksack. As he opened it, Jack caught the odour of God knew what. Drug money sure enough.

'It's all here. He'll probably have a note counter. Depends on where you meet and how long he wants to spend in your company.' Charlie dipped his hand into the rucksack and brought out a small metal box. Opening it up, Jack saw two small test tubes and a small metal spoon. This is your tester. If it turns red then all is okay. Pink and it's shit. I'm only interested in red. Test two batches if you can. He'll expect that.'

He clicked the cover shut and handed the case to Jack. 'Good luck. I think you'll need it. I'll call you as soon as he calls me with the venue. Ring me when you complete the deal and we can meet up. You don't want to be in possession of class A drugs for too long, do you?'

Jack didn't even cast a glance at him as he opened the door. 'I'll wait for your call.'

Chapter Forty-Six

Rico had visited the offices of London Elite off Bond Street and paid for the hire of the suite in cash. It was off Dover Street in Mayfair and he went round to scope it out as soon as he was given the rental documents. The doorman looked to be around sixty with a careworn face. He smiled at Rico and gave the documents a cursory glance.

'Looks fine to me, sir. I would think your rooms are being prepared as we speak. Were you hoping to see them now?'

'Yes, if possible. It's an important business meeting and I want everything to be right.' Rico palmed the man a twenty and saw a nod in return.

'I'll just make a phone call, sir. Please give me a minute.'

Rico stepped back and watched him as he spoke into a cream-coloured phone.

'Your suite will be ready in a few minutes, sir. Let me show you where the lifts are.'

'Thank you. What is your name by the way?'

'I'm George.'

'Pleased to meet you, George. You are very good at your job. Thank you for your help.'

'My pleasure.'

'Tell me, if I had a visiting business client who wished to leave the building in shall we say a discreet way, would this be possible?'

'Of course. I'll accompany you up to your suite and show you.'

The phone rang on George's desk and he nodded to Rico as he listened.

'Right, sir, we can go up now.'

They travelled up in the lift at a comfortable high speed and stopped at the fifteenth floor.

'Here we are. I'll show you to your suite and the other lift. Just follow me.'

Rico followed as George pointed to a door numbered 1560.

'That's your one. Got a nice view over London.' Then he ushered him down the thickly-carpeted corridor. 'This is the service lift. Because we have such a turnover of agency cleaning staff there is no security code. Just press the button and the lift will come. I'm afraid it ends up in the basement and the exit leads onto a back alley. It is not very pleasant.'

'Please don't worry about that, George. It's a small price to pay for total discretion when big business rivals meet, but don't want others to know.'

'That's good. I must get back to the desk, sir.'

'Of course. And thank you for your help.'

Rico used his key card and entered the suite. The first thing he noticed was the large picture window and tasteful furnishings in the large slightly L-shaped room. A bar with two high stools had been built into one corner. It was carpeted in a plush burgundy colour. Rico smiled as he thought how apt that choice would become. A grand white marble fireplace occupied the far wall and there were several paintings on the walls depicting typical English country scenes. Opening the door on the opposite side to the fireplace, Rico found himself in a sumptuous bedroom with a cream and grey theme. Another door led to the en-suite bathroom with white fittings and a huge walk-in shower.

He returned to the living room and sat down on the large black leather sofa. As he looked around he began to envisage his plan of action when Charlie arrived in the room. Sticking his hand into his rucksack he brought out the small serrated knife and placed it under the cushion he was sitting on. Placing his rucksack next to the sofa, he looked across to a black leather armchair and rose from his seat. Turning the armchair round slightly, he faced it to the picture window where the piercing light would be streaming in later in the afternoon. Charlie's seat.

He checked his watch and it said 11am. He had two items still to purchase and after letting himself out, he took the lift to the ground floor and waved to George. 'See you later.'

Chapter Forty-Seven

Eva picked up Jack's call on the third ring and said, 'Hi, Jack.'

'Hi, Eva good to hear your voice.'

'I wondered what you were up to today?'

Jack paused before answering. 'I've a difficult day ahead.'

'Oh. I'm coming up to central London and wondered if you'd like a quick lunch between my meetings?'

'That would be great. It will have to be a bit short but I'll tell you all about it when we meet. Would Covent Garden be any good for you?'

'That would be fine for me.'

'I know a nice little restaurant there. How about 12.30 at Covent Garden Tube station?'

'That's a date. I'll see you later. Bye, Jack.'

He heard her blow a kiss just before the line went dead.

As he sat on the Tube train he kept his rucksack with the money on his lap. He decided to tell Eva about his meeting with Rico, but minimise the risks involved. He wouldn't lie to her, but knew there was no point in alarming her. For all he knew, Rico might not make the call to Charlie.

Jack arrived first and stood outside the station. The street was packed with tourists and office workers on their lunch break. He felt a tap on his shoulder and turned to see Eva. She looked striking in her dark business suit and he kissed her before giving her a big hug.

'That's some welcome, Jack. What's in the rucksack?'

'A lot of money.'

Eva laughed as if she didn't believe him so he left it there.

'It's good to see you, Eva. A lovely surprise. I didn't expect to see you today.'

She linked her arm through his as they headed into Covent Garden. As they passed the street statues, one of them covered completely in silver caught Eva's eye.

'How do they do it? It's as if they are suspended in thin air.'

Suddenly, the statue lunged and Eva let out a scream. Everyone around burst out laughing and Jack tossed a pound coin into the box. They were both smiling as they walked on and Jack pointed to a side street, steering Eva in its direction.

The restaurant was a few yards down on the left and as they sat down to look at the menu, Jack ordered a bottle of sparkling water.

'It's just us, Jack. How about switching our phones off for half an hour?'

'I can't, Eva. I may get an important call.'

'More important than me?'

'No, but I need to take it.'

They both ordered salads and after the waiter left, Eva covered Jack's hand with hers. 'What's up, Jack?'

'It's a big day. I am due to meet up with Rico and take a load of bad drugs off the street.'

'Oh, my God, are you serious?'

'Well, yes. Why the surprise?'

'Well, from what you've told me, he's the top man and ruthless. Why would he want to meet with you anyway?'

'He doesn't know it's going to be me. He thinks he's meeting Charlie. After the deal he'll be arrested with the money.'

Just as he tried to read into her reaction the waiter arrived with the salads. Jack looked into Eva's face but saw nothing but concern and fear.

'Will you have people with you, Jack?'

'The police will be close by. I'll have plenty of help, so don't worry. I'll be fine.

She grimaced. 'It doesn't stop me worrying.'

They began eating their salads, but Jack's thoughts on his meeting with Rico played in his mind. They were interrupted when his phone rang. It said 'Charlie' and Jack hit the green button.

'I've just had the call from Rico. It's going to be in Mayfair, just off Brook Street. He wouldn't give me the exact address and said he'd phone ten minutes ahead of the meeting. Told me to be close by and he'd call ten minutes ahead of the meet.'

'Okay. I'll be in position for 3.30pm. Call me when you have the exact address.'

'I will.'

'That was the call, Eva. I need to be leaving quite soon.'

'I don't want you to go.'

'I have to do this and it'll be all over by the end of the afternoon. I'll call you and come to your place tonight.'

'That would be lovely. I can't wait for this to finish. Just call me when you can. I'll be thinking of you all the time now.'

Jack called for the bill and they made their way outside. As they were bumped along by the ever-growing crowds, Jack held tightly to his rucksack. Eva rested her head on Jack's shoulder when they arrived back at the station. They flagged taxis and Jack kissed her before he was driven off clutching the rucksack. Looking back he saw the worried look on Eva's face as she watched him until he was out of sight.

He called Matt and told him the venue was off Brook Street in Mayfair.

'I'm going to be there at three-thirty. I'll call you again when I arrive. Will you be there?'

'Yes. I'm going to let you know how we are going to back you up. Are you sure you want to go through with this?'

'Yeah, I'm sure.'

Chapter Forty-Eight

Rico returned to the suite at 3pm and began unpacking and charging his two mobiles. The cocaine was packed into a narrow plastic bag, making it more difficult to dig down for a sample. The top layer was medium to high grade, but lower down there was a heavy concentration of benzocaine, baking soda and fentanyl. All sorts of shit. Rico didn't want Charlie to be hanging around for longer than necessary and he was bound to have told someone where their meeting was. He wanted the money and to be out of the building in the shortest time. He'd be in a taxi to Heathrow before Charlie got back home to start digging down to the bottom of the bag.

He phoned down to reception.

'Hi, George. My first guest should be here in about half an hour. Would you give me a call when he arrives and just show him to the lift? I'll meet him on this floor.'

'Of course, sir.'

Checking the sofa, he reminded himself where the small knife was tucked under the cushion. Charlie's chair was just at the right angle for the sun to stream into his eyes. He took a last look into the rucksack and checked that the drugs, bag, rope and duct tape were inside, then placed it on the floor next to where he would be sitting. It was now 3.40 and he would ring Charlie in ten minutes with the exact address and instructions for entry to the building.

***

Jack sat in a small coffee shop just round the corner from Brook Street and waited for Charlie's call. It came at 3.50 and he sounded nervous.

'Jack, it's Charlie.'

'I know, what are the instructions?'

'He's in Sovereign House.'

'I've just walked past it. What did he say?'

'It was a very quick call. He told me to go in and present myself to the guy on reception and say he was expected in suite 1560 at 4 o'clock. He said to announce myself as Charlie. He also said to make sure I was on my own.'

'That was it?'

'Yeah, that's all he said. The call lasted about thirty seconds.'

'Okay. Where are you?'

'I'm at home.'

'I'll call you when this is through.'

'Good luck, Jack.'

'Yeah.'

Jack called Matt. 'I'll have to be quick. It's room 1560 of Sovereign House in Mayfair.' He recounted the conversation with Charlie and then said, 'I'm going in now.'

'Watch your back, Jack.'

He walked out into the street and slung the rucksack over his shoulder. Entering the reception area just before 4 o'clock he made his way to the male receptionist.

'Hi. I have an appointment at 4 o'clock in Room 1560.'

'Name, sir?'

'Charlie.'

'Just one second.' George picked up the desk phone and after a couple of seconds said, 'Your 4 o'clock appointment is here sir.' Turning back to Jack, he said, 'Would you like to follow me?'

They waited for the lift and when the doors opened George pressed 15. 'You will be met outside the lift.'

Jack hardly had time to collect his thoughts as the lift move swiftly and silently upwards. There was a 'ding' when it reached the fifteenth floor and Jack looked left and right before stepping out. To his right about twenty yards away stood the man he recognised as Rico. He turned his jacket collar up, stepped out and began walking towards him. As he neared, Rico pointed him towards the open door of his suite.

'Go in. There's no one else here.'

Jack kept his eye on him as he passed by and walked into the room. He turned as Rico closed the door.

'So, Charlie, you have the money?'

Jack nodded as Rico showed him to a chair near the centre of the room.

'Have a seat and let's get this done as quickly as we can. We'll lay our phones on the table for safety. Okay?'

Rico placed his phone on the coffee table and Jack followed suit.

The dipping afternoon sun was shining straight into his eyes and Jack quickly shifted position on the armchair. He saw Rico sit down on the sofa next to a rucksack resting on the floor.

'How about we open our rucksacks on the carpet.' Rico made it a statement rather than a question and Jack just shrugged.

Jack looked at Rico and said, 'It's all in here in the denominations you requested. Check it if you like. I'm in the cocaine business, nothing else.'

Rico said nothing before opening his rucksack to reveal the bag of white powder with the testing paraphernalia sitting on top. He pulled everything out and closed the flap of the rucksack.

Jack knew there had to be something else hidden in there as the bag had been sitting too high inside it.

'Okay, Rico how do you want to play it? Here's the money. Count it if you like. It's all there.'

Jack picked up one of the test tube kits and opened the bag. With a small spoon he scooped some of the powder and emptied it in. Shaking it up he waited and the liquid turned red.

'One more and we are good to go.' He opened the second testing tube and dug down again with the spoon. The liquid turned as red as the first and Jack nodded to Rico.

'Looks okay. Count the money.'

He watched as Rico placed a wad into the note counter and pressed a button. There was an air of tension now and after three wads Rico just said, 'It's there.'

Jack passed over the rest of the money and Rico held out the bag of cocaine.

'We have a deal, Charlie.' As he said it, one of the phones rang and Rico looked down to see Jack's phone flashing. The name said 'Eva'.

They both stared at the phone as it rang out. Jack watched and waited to see if the name registered with him.

Rico leapt up with a knife in his right hand. 'You're the private detective. What the fuck are you doing here? Where's Charlie?'

'Charlie is indisposed.'

'What does that mean?'

'He couldn't make it, so he sent me.'

'Don't fuck with me. Are you on your own?'

'Yes, only Charlie knows I'm here.'

'Big mistake.'

'You killed Susan Long, didn't you.'

Rico sneered. 'I'm told it was an accident. Who cares?'

'I know she was involved with your organisation from her phone records. You knew what was going on.'

'There's a heavy price to pay for stupidity in my organisation. As far as I know, her death was due to a random accident.'

Jack looked at him and wondered how far he could go. 'How can a dead man jump out of a window?'

'This Susan was in the wrong place at the wrong time. Shit happens. I can't help you.'

Snapping back, Jack spat out, 'You're dealing in fentanyl. You and your organisation are killing young people.'

'So, what? I'm not interested, but prove it.'

'I'm holding the proof in this bag.'

'Fuck you.'

Rico stuck his hand down the side of the seat and brought out his knife and lunged at Jack. As he tried to dodge the blade it caught Jack on the side of his neck. He immediately felt a searing pain, and warm liquid started running down his neck. He saw Rico coming for him again and managed to clutch at a cushion and bring it in front of his body to block the next blow. Feeling his vision fading, he rolled across the sofa as Rico dived at him. He fell onto the floor and brought his legs up and managed to kick Rico in the groin as he made another lunge with the knife. Jack took hold of the base of a lamp next to the sofa and as it came crashing down, Rico tripped on the wire leading to the side wall. As Rico landed on the floor there was a loud banging on the door. Rico propped himself up and kicked Jack hard in the ribs.

Jack pushed himself backwards to put some space between them and began to feel dizzy. He saw Rico stumble towards the door and shout, 'Who is it?'

'It's me. George.'

'What do you want?'

'You need to come out quickly.'

Rico opened the door a few of inches as Jack was trying to focus on what was happening, when he heard a series of loud bangs. As the blackness began to descend, he saw Rico falling backwards, the front of his shirt turning red from a massive wound in his chest. A young man with a hand gun stepped over Rico's still form as he came towards him. Tony Northwood calmly stuck the gun back inside his black leather jacket and knelt beside him. Jack didn't hear Tony shouting, 'Speak to me, Jack.'

Chapter Forty-Nine

Much of Mayfair had been effectively closed off as armed police swarmed into Sovereign House. Police cars, ambulances and two fire engines blocked the street outside, with blue strobe lights piercing the late afternoon gloom. The wailing of sirens filled the air as the emergency response continued. The closure had quickly led to gridlock in the whole of west London. Residents were being escorted outside from the building and people were running away from the area as rumour spread about a crazed gunman on the loose. Although only a block away, Matt's journey was slow due to the traffic chaos but as he eventually arrived at Sovereign House he made his way quickly to the fifteenth floor. He watched in horror as Jack was wheeled out by paramedics. He was on a drip and the trolley was being pushed towards the lift at a quick pace.

As Matt entered room 1560, he immediately saw the large dark stain on the carpet just inside the door, with another next to the sofa. The empty packaging and general detritus left after a major trauma was scattered all over the floor. Two other medics were kneeling by Rico and as one of them got up, Matt went over to him.

'Were you tending the other victim?'

'Yes, I was.'

'Can you tell me how he is?'

'It's bad. Knife wound trauma to his neck with substantial blood loss. Another centimetre and it would have been the jugular.'

'Will he come through?'

'Impossible to say at this stage. The next twenty-four hours will tell us a lot. He's been taken to St. Thomas's.'

Matt looked down at Rico's body. 'How many bullets did this one take?'

'Four in the chest. Wouldn't have known much.'

'Pity.'

As the CSI team began moving around and forensics began their ritual checks, Matt took a last look at the scene. He saw the two rucksacks on the floor and a bag of white powder on the coffee table. He made a mental note to ask how much fentanyl had been cut into the cocaine. The drug that had killed so many had now led to the death of the dealer himself and the irony wasn't lost on him as he made his way towards the door. He needed to speak to the receptionist to find out how much he knew.

***

Eva's mobile rang at 5.30pm when she was still at her desk.

'Eva, it's Matt, Jack's friend from the police.'

She froze as she heard his voice.

'I'm afraid Jack has been hurt quite badly and he is in St Thomas's Hospital. I'm so sorry to give you this news. I'm going to send a car for you if you can let me know where you are.'

Eva started to shake and she thought she was going to be sick. 'Oh, God, no! No! What's happened?'

'He's been cut on the neck with a knife and has lost a lot of blood. We got to him quickly and he was blue lighted to hospital. He's in intensive care and we are waiting for news.'

'I'm still at the office. I need to get to him.'

'Just give me your address, Eva and we'll be with you in a few minutes.'

She closed down her laptop and grabbed her things before running for the door. A police car arrived at the front of the offices in what seemed like an instant and a uniformed officer opened the door for her.

'Do you know how he is?' she asked.

'I'm sorry ma'am, we haven't any update, but we'll get you to him as soon as we possibly can. Please fasten your seat belt.'

Eva couldn't believe the speed at which the car was driven through the streets. The noise of the siren was almost deafening, but she just wanted to get there. She felt in a daze as she ran into the hospital entrance. A police officer followed her and they made their way to reception.

***

Matt began reading the reports of the shooting at Sovereign House. The suite had been booked through an agency with cash and the name Mr. Alvarez had been used. The duration of the rental was a maximum of five hours, which was apparently not unusual for business meetings. CCTV was available showing the renter when visiting the agency to pay cash for the booking. The receptionist at Sovereign House, one George Fenton was suffering from shock but had said that a young man had approached him at 4.20pm and said he was a courier and had a confidential document for suite 1560. His instructions were explicit and it had to be slipped noiselessly under the door. Matt realised that this was probably Tony Northwood. As he read the report, he realised how much Jack wanted justice for his client and Rebecca. He'd put his life on the line to nail the top man in the organisation. Picking up his phone, he rang St. Thomas's.

Chapter Fifty

Eva stayed all night at the hospital and kept herself awake with cups of black coffee. She had never felt so scared in her life. As she thought back to all the time she'd spent with Jack in Spain she couldn't ever have imagined this happening. Her mind was racing as she reflected on the day's events. She wondered if there was a reckless side to Jack she'd never known about. He'd put himself in mortal danger maybe because of her, and the shock and panic it had caused was making her feel ill. If Jack was to be in constant danger as a P. I. she knew she would find it difficult to live with the worry. Eva knew she was in love with him but the life he led and the people he had to deal with frightened her. His world was so alien to hers and she wondered if she could cope with the constant worry of it all. The last few weeks had shaken her and now the reality was brutality and death.

***

The news from the doctors looking after Jack was cautious. He'd suffered massive blood loss and there were possible complications, but he was responding to treatment and they would know more in a few hours.

Matt had received the information with huge relief and just wanted to see his old friend. He had asked for reports on the contents of the cocaine that Rico had carried to Sovereign House and the results were devastating for potential weekend users. It had been cut so badly that anyone who had bought from the batch could have died. The small amount of street-level cocaine had been cut with at least three additives plus fentanyl to give it the feeling of being the real stuff. As Matt read the report, he realised the appalling risk that cocaine users were putting themselves at. Everything was changing.

Chapter Fifty-One

When he finally awoke, Jack's head ached and his mouth was dry. He had the urge to be sick, but when it didn't actually happen he tried to relax. He could see a couple of nurses in the corner of his right eye but couldn't work out why they were there. There was a pain coming from his head but it wasn't bad enough to shout out. He looked down and saw all sorts of contraptions attached to him and became even more puzzled. He must have made some sort of noise because one of the nurses came over to him.

'Hello. How are you feeling?'

'Where am I?'

'You're in hospital. You've had an injury to your neck. We're going to look after you.'

He whispered, 'How is Eva?'

'She's fine. She's spent the night here and you can see her soon.'

Jack couldn't quite work out what was going on but began dozing off as he was about to ask another question.

'Everything is going to be okay,' the nurse reassured him. 'Just try to rest.'

He dozed off again, his mind a blank canvas.

***

Eva spent three days in or near St Thomas's and was eventually allowed to be with Jack at his bedside.

'I love you, Jack,' were her first words to him. He managed a weak smile in response as she held his hand.

She had constantly bombarded the staff with questions and most of the answers had been guarded.

'It'll take time.'

'It is a big injury.'

'We'll know more soon.'

Eva took it all as positive and began planning for Jack's recovery. She didn't know what the future held for them, but he was sure to like everything she'd planned. Well, she hoped he would.

***

165

It had been six days since his injury and the doctors said he was making good progress. Eva had told him that she'd spoken with the consultant and it had been agreed he would probably be released in the next few days. Just a few final tests. 'We'll get him up and about just to make sure he can move around without danger,' the doctor had said. 'He mustn't be left on his own in the first few days.'

'Don't worry, he won't be.'

As she bent over to kiss him, she gave him the good news. 'When can I get out of here?' he asked.

'You'll be out very soon.'

'Maybe you could put me up for a few days. Keep me out of trouble.'

She laughed and held his hand. 'I'd like that.'

'I don't want to put you through this again, Eva.' He saw the tears forming in her eyes and squeezed her hand before pulling her down to sit on the bed. He kissed her and said, 'I've done a lot of thinking as I've lain here and I don't want to lose you, Eva. I think I need a change of occupation.'

She kissed him back and whispered, 'I never want to lose you either.'

Chapter Fifty-Two

Convalescing at Eva's, Jack began using light weights to regain upper body strength, and daily walks around the local park helped relieve the boredom. A week had passed when Matt rang him as he was returning from his afternoon stroll.

'Jack, how are you?'

'I'm doing well. Strength coming back and beginning to feel normal again. Eva keeps me on a tight leash. How are you?'

'All well, but too busy. I'd like to come and see you. Would that be allowed?'

Jack laughed. 'Of course, but no grapes.'

'Just so you know, we're about to arrest Charlie for possession and trafficking of class A drugs, but I thought it could be useful if we had a talk first. I need some extra background.'

'Good. I'm pleased to hear that. Another drug-dealing scumbag off the streets is always good news.' Jack cleared his throat before asking, 'I'd like to meet Tony soon. Is that possible?'

'Maybe, but not just yet. I was coming to Tony. He's still in custody and his solicitor is trying for bail because of the circumstances, but at the end of the day he killed with pre-meditation.'

'Yeah, but he was met at the door by a guy with a bloodied knife in his hand.'

'We could talk about that when we meet.'

'How is he in himself?'

'He's doing okay. We're working on how he got the gun. He found out the meeting place at Sovereign House from Charlie. Tony convinced him it would help him get closure if he stood outside and watched it all go down, and Charlie fell for it.'

As Jack walked back to Eva's flat he said, 'Let me get back to you, Matt. Probably be in the morning after I've spoken with Eva. Great to hear from you.'

'And you, pal. Take it easy.'

When Eva arrived home from work, Jack had prepared a meal of meat balls and spaghetti and had opened a bottle of red wine. Everything was laid on the table.

'I could get used to this, Jack,' she said, giving him a gentle kiss. 'How's your day been?'

'Good. I walked three miles and met a few dog walkers. Matt rang me and wants to meet up.'

Eva grimaced. 'You're still convalescing.'

'I know, but it's just a quick one. They need some details on Charlie from me. I also said I'd like to meet Tony.'

'How is he?'

'Okay, but still in custody. I need to thank him, you know. He saved my life and when he comes to court, I want to stand up and remind everyone of that.'

Eva dropped another kiss on his cheek. 'Just don't rush into things.'

'I won't.'

Chapter Fifty-Three

Jack and Matt met up at The Angel pub in Clapham.

'Good to see you, Jack. You look well.'

'I am. Eva's taking good care of me. I'm ready to go back to work, but I need clearance from the consultant first. I've been very lucky.'

They ordered from the lunch menu and Matt began talking.

Jack stopped him and said, 'Before you start I need to know about any charges against Eva.'

Matt replied immediately, 'There are none and there is no evidence at all that Eva knew anything about Susan's involvement with drugs. The Spanish police have questioned Vicente at great length and it is now accepted that his allegations about Eva were completely false. He was pointing the finger at anyone in the hope it would help him. I'm sorry it happened, Jack but it had to be followed up.'

'I know and I'm very pleased it's settled. I never had any doubts and if anything, it brought Eva and me even closer. What about Charlie?'

'We believe we have enough surveillance evidence on him to bring charges and we're about to set up an undercover drug bust. He's so greedy he's bound to bite and we'll catch him in the act. He's dealing seven days a week and doesn't go to the bank. He must be wading through banknotes at home. Was he aggressive when you were dealing with him? Any guns?'

Jack sipped his glass of water and shook his head. 'No, quite the opposite actually. The most unlikely drug dealer. It was as if he was selling bags of sweeties. He spends lots of time in car parks buying and selling and his market seems to be middle-class users. I think he believes it's all quite innocent because everyone's doing it, so it must be okay.'

'Well, he made a big mistake when he supplied youngsters at that rave in Oxfordshire. I'll keep you posted on the arrest. If he's found guilty, he's almost bound to do heavy time.'

Jack asked about Tony.

'Tony is still in custody. It's a tricky one. His solicitor is saying he only carried the gun in case he needed to defend himself and he finished up having to. The fact that Rico was brandishing the knife when he opened the door is likely to be his best line of defence. Tony has a lot going for him, but he had a gun and that's the elephant in the room.'

Jack asked, 'Do you know where he got hold of it?'

'He says he bought it on the dark web. That's all we know right now. His solicitor says he'll be able to give us more detail later and he's being very co-operative with us. I'm hopeful he'll get a lenient sentence. He can't forgive himself over Rebecca's death but he probably saved countless lives by killing Rico. I'm hopeful the jury will see it that way.'

The waitress arrived with their lunches and they both stopped talking for a couple of minutes as they began eating.

Matt took a break from his chilli con carne and said, 'I'm pleased you and Eva are getting it together. You need someone to share the ups and downs. Especially the downs in our business.'

'You're right. She's lovely and I'm lucky to have met her. I don't think she wants me working in this profession anymore and I can't say I blame her. I have some big decisions to make, because things are changing out there.'

Matt leaned across and said, 'The drug scene is almost out of control now. What you did was dangerous, but we'll take out a lot of dealers when we arrest Charlie. We're sure he'll give up names in the hope of a lighter sentence. He has tried to make out he's just helping the middle classes to enjoy their weekends, but the death rate inside the gangs is escalating and youngsters are being recruited to build new business outside of London. Profits are incredible and life is cheap. A nosy P.I.'s life is even cheaper. Stay in the investigation business if you want, but think about what you take on, Jack, because Eva is right.'

Jack rested his knife and fork, sat back and said, 'I know.'

Chapter Fifty-Four

They sat at the table in Eva's kitchen and she asked Jack about his meeting with Matt.

'It was good to see him and we had a bit to catch up on. He offered me some advice.'

'You're not good at taking advice.'

'I know, but this time I'm actually going to take it. I'm going to look for a regular job.'

'Really?'

'Yep. I don't want to put you through any of this again. But you've got to accept that I may become boring.'

'Jack, you'll never be that. Do you mean it about your work?'

'I'll see out my caseload and then look to doing something different. Maybe some high-end security work. It can pay well.'

They lifted their glasses and clinked them.

'It's a deal,' said Eva. 'I love you.

'I love you too.'

***

Jack and Eva were married at Marylebone Registry Office with family and close friends present.

They spent their honeymoon in Sorrento with a sea view room overlooking the Bay of Naples.

Jack is still working out his caseload.